A VERY SPECIAL YEAR

On a quiet back street in a sleepy town, there sits an old bookshop: an emporium of reading delights. Inside, there sits a most peculiar novel — its ending changes depending on the reader . . . For young Valerie, who has just inherited the shop after the sudden (and very mysterious) disappearance of her Aunt Charlotte, the place amounts to nothing more than a badly-run business, to be whipped into shape before being sold on. But when an enigmatic customer appears and enquires about the novel with no ending, the magic of the place is unlocked . . .

SPECIA ~~)ERS~~

THE ULVERSCROFT FOUNDATION
(registered UK charity number 264873)

was ~~e~~ A⌐⌐⊃ ⌐r
~~researcl~~  ~~ses.~~
E⌐
the Ulverscroft Foundation a⌐⌐⌐

- The Children's Eye Unit at Moorfields Eye Hospital, London
- The Ulverscroft Children's Eye Unit at Great Ormond Street Hospital for Sick Children
- Funding research into eye diseases and treatment at the Department of Ophthalmology, University of Leicester
- The Ulverscroft Vision Research Group, Institute of Child Health
- Twin operating theatres at the Western Ophthalmic Hospital, London
- The Chair of Ophthalmology at the Royal Australian College of Ophthalmologists

You can help further the work of the Foundation by making a donation or leaving a legacy. Every contribution is gratefully received. If you would like to help support the Foundation or require further information, please contact:

THE ULVERSCROFT FOUNDATION
**The Green, Bradgate Road, Anstey
Leicester LE7 7FU, England
Tel: (0116) 236 4325**

website: www.foundation.ulverscroft.com

Thomas Montasser has worked as a journalist and university lecturer, and was a director of a small theatre in Munich. He is a literary agent, and likes nothing better than rummaging around in small bookshops. A father of three children, he lives with his family in Bavaria, Germany.

THOMAS MONTASSER

A VERY SPECIAL YEAR

Translated from the German by Jamie Bulloch

Complete and Unabridged

ULVERSCROFT
Leicester

First published in Great Britain in 2016 by
Oneworld Publications
London

First Large Print Edition
published 2017
by arrangement with
Oneworld Publications
London

A catalogue record for this book is available
from the British Library.

ISBN 978–1–4448–3337–9

Published by
F. A. Thorpe (Publishing)
Anstey, Leicestershire

Set by Words & Graphics Ltd.
Anstey, Leicestershire
Printed and bound in Great Britain by
T. J. International Ltd., Padstow, Cornwall

For Mariam,
the muse of my budding dreams

*Reality can't compete
with literature,
you see.*

Valerie's mother

*A book is so much more
than the sum of its words!*

Noé

1

If someone had peered through the window, that person would have glimpsed little more than the bent back of a carefully dressed elderly lady, whose snow-white, somewhat tousled bun was hovering above the till, bathed in the gentle light of a tired ceiling lamp. Maybe that person would have seen her emphatically draw a line below a list she'd written in an ancient notebook, then snap shut said notebook no less emphatically and snap open a handbag beside her, from which she took a purse, and from this she slipped out a rather low-value banknote and placed it in the till. That person would have seen her slender hand, dotted with age spots, but otherwise aristocratic and pale, close the till and touch it again — as you might comfort an old friend with a slap on the shoulder — before she finally stood up, conducted an inspection of the floor-to-ceiling shelves, whispered something to them, then turned off the light and left the small shop via the back door. Thus our observer would have been the witness of a specific event that can be summed up in two words: Charlotte's disappearance.

Now, you don't need to be especially perceptive to realize that no such observer existed. On that — significant, as we shall see later — winter evening no one was passing by to glance through the window or, more accurately, at the window display. In other words, it was a perfectly normal evening, a typical evening rather than an unusual one. On no account could you blame this on a lack of people milling about; on the contrary, the old lady's shop, although slightly set back from the street, was located in an area with a good level of footfall, as people put it so nicely. A bakery would have probably done a roaring trade, an off-licence too, not to mention a fitness studio. In this respect, the elderly lady, whom our non-existent observer would have seen at the beginning, had a more difficult job. Much more difficult. For, as we know, passing trade is an odd species: wilful, stubborn, unpredictable, but most of all, never there when you need it. For the sake of accuracy, however, we must note that the business this elderly lady was in depends far more on regular customers than passing trade. For it doesn't offer mass-produced goods for swift consumption or dubious, rapidly fading beauty, but something considerably more substantial, important even. We are talking here about being or not being, in more than one

2

sense. Which is why Charlotte's disappearance can quite rightly be regarded as a cultural event, albeit not a pleasant one. But more on that later.

It would be a while before the door to the small shop was opened again. And under very different circumstances.

2

The paint was peeling in places and there was a crack in one corner of the glass pane in the door. Valerie shook her head. When she finally managed to open the antiquated lock — it had slightly rusted and the door was jammed at the top — she was hit by weeks-old stale air. Leaving the door open, she headed straight for the office at the back to open the window there too. Fortunately it was a warm spring day.

Valerie dropped her bag on the floor and tried not to fall immediately into despair. Where on earth to begin? This shop was like a dress that the elderly woman had tailored to fit her life. It may now have fitted her perfectly, but for Valerie's youthful existence it was uncomfortable, shapeless and wholly impractical. She sat down hesitantly on the worn armchair, which Aunt Charlotte had positioned by the window for the light. 'What *have* I let myself in for?' she sighed.

On the little side table lay a pile of business cards with the shop's name in elegantly flowing letters. Valerie picked up one; it radiated a particularly magical aura. The surface felt as if it had been coated with velvet, the letters were embossed in a deep, dark red. Valerie was unable to suppress a smile. 'Ringelnatz & Co.,' she said softly, with a mixture of hilarity and embarrassment. Evidently Aunt Charlotte had been trying to emulate the Paris bookshop she so admired: Shakespeare & Co. Valerie couldn't understand why she hadn't at least called her shop something like Goethe & Co. But perhaps there was no need to understand. Perhaps it was simply because Aunt Charlotte was from another era.

So, the bookshop. How long was it since she'd last been here? Years. Several. Since her mother died, she hadn't seen much of her aunt; Papa and Charlotte had never really got on. As a professor of economics, his conversation would soon turn to business matters. Aunt Charlotte exasperated him. 'Can't you get it into your head that you're no businesswoman?' he'd exclaim, literally every time they spoke, and turn away shaking his head. The two of them had nothing in common.

And now, of all people, it was up to Valerie to liquidate the old bookshop where she'd spent so many happy hours of her childhood, and whose outdatedness she later found so alien. Chance had decreed that she should be the elderly lady's closest relative and that, with her recent degree in business administration, she should also have the necessary know-how for the job. It was just that she'd set herself other goals for this post-degree period. She had already enrolled on a master's degree, without which she wouldn't be able to set herself up for a career as a consultant specializing in Scandinavia and the emerging economies of the Baltic. As she sat here in Aunt Charlotte's old bookshop, two dozen applications were on their way to top firms: business consultancies, accountancy firms, marketing agencies and think tanks. This is where she wanted to go, into the heart of things, where business was pulsing, where brainstorms thundered and the future was being invented. Instead, she was stranded here amid reams of old paper. Moreover, she fancied she had some idea of what awaited her in her aunt's accounts. That's to say, she had no idea; it was something she would only discover when she was right in the middle of this story. If not later.

★ ★ ★

The situation was further complicated by the fact that although Aunt Charlotte had disappeared, she had not been registered as dead. She had merely not been found anywhere. There was as little evidence that she had willingly gone somewhere as there was that she had unwillingly arrived somewhere — even if this destination were the afterlife. But nobody, of course, was under any illusion, least of all Valerie. She'd always liked Aunt Charlotte and she was very saddened that the elderly lady — she would have been pushing eighty — had departed this life in such a mysterious way. There had been no sightings of her; she had quite simply taken leave of her existence, which was as cranky as it was convivial. And the note that had been found on her kitchen table was not even valid as an official will because it lacked a signature and it didn't refer in so many words to anyone actually *inheriting* her estate, but maintaining it: 'My niece Valerie is to look after everything.' That was all.

The shop probably hadn't changed since its foundation in the late 1950s. True, different books adorned the shelves now and the samovar had only arrived in the nineties — by chance Valerie knew exactly when — after a trip her aunt had made to post-communist Russia, the land of Dostoevsky, Tolstoy and Pushkin. Russia had been Charlotte's dream destination, at least until that visit, which had brought some sober reality (back then, Mama had said, 'Reality can't compete with literature, you see.'). But apart from this, there were floor-to-ceiling wooden shelves that could have done with a polish years ago, a worn parquet floor, three lamps with ancient green shades on wobbly side tables and a heavy, gathered curtain with gold embroidery at the edges, which separated the display window from the rest of the shop and which had once probably been a stage curtain, maybe even in the pre-war era.

The post-war era, when Aunt Charlotte had opened her bookshop, cannot have been a bad time to earn money from printed matter. After all, people had been starved culturally and intellectually, and were longing for good stories and clever ideas. In theory, the right business idea, Valerie thought — for back then. The problem was that the elderly lady had not moved with the times; on the contrary, in all those years essentially nothing had changed. Her trade had been overtaken by the professionalism of modern business ideas and the glamour of new media. I mean, who seriously still read books these days?

A clock hung above the entrance, and Valerie was truly astounded that it hadn't stopped, just as time had stopped here many years ago. A quarter to eleven. And not a customer in sight. 'Ringelnatz & Co.,' Valerie repeated with a sigh, heading to the small room at the back, which was reached via two steps and also separated from the shop by a gathered curtain — perhaps the rest of the large stage curtain framing the display window. The cash till seemed to have been pilfered from a film from the 1930s; large and black, it stood on the desk, yet it shone with promise. It was empty, of course. Or at least almost empty. The drawer contained a ten-euro note plus a few unsorted coins, which, added up, wouldn't come to much. On the right of the desk was a small cabinet that reminded Valerie of the catalogue in the old section of her university library; to the left lay a well-thumbed notebook, which at first glance revealed itself to be the cash account book. 'Aha,' Valerie muttered. 'So you kept some accounts at least.' A glimmer of hope, that things might not prove to be so dire, sparked inside her, just bright enough to last for a couple of minutes before dissipating as a lost illusion. 'OK, that can't really be it,' Valerie concluded and decided to fortify herself with a coffee, amending her decision when she discovered that evidently there'd been no place for coffee in Aunt Charlotte's realm. With some difficulty she got the samovar going and waited.

A samovar consists of a large water boiler,

on which a small pot sits that you fill with tea leaves and then pour in boiling water from the lower vessel. The pot is then returned to its place until the tea has brewed to such a strength that more or less homeopathic measures can be dribbled into a cup and mixed with more boiling water to reach the correct blend. This process takes the time you might expect, which is why Valerie spent longer waiting than she'd planned. So she plucked a book almost at random from the shelves and sat back down in Aunt Charlotte's chair to leaf through it.

'Chapter One' began with an arrival, as do so many books, and as Valerie's story did, too, at least in relation to her elderly aunt's bookshop. But if we're being precise, it was much later in the day:

> *It was late evening when Josef K arrived. The village lay in deep snow. Nothing could be seen of the hill on which the castle stood; it was sur- rounded by fog and darkness. Not even a weak glimmer of light hinted at the presence of the large castle. K stood for a long while on the wooden bridge that led from the country road to the village, gazing up into the apparent void . . .*

A good samovar has a mechanism that automatically switches off the boiler if it heats the water for too long — although you ought to know that samovars are designed to simmer away for ages. Charlotte's samovar would also have possessed such a mechanism, but it came from post-Soviet Russia, a time when shoddy manufacturing no longer induced the wrath of the state apparatus, nor yet the wrath of the consumer. So the water kept boiling and boiling until on page 248 a card fell into Valerie's lap and she looked up in astonishment.

Dusk had set in outside. The balmy trace of spring had long given way to a perfidious draught which got the better of her nose before she realized it. As the day departed the sniffles appeared and the tea steeped in its pot, while for the first time ever Valerie read a Franz Kafka novel. It took her completely by surprise, for with each page she turned she kept expecting to get bored.

The aforementioned card turned out to be an order form on which Aunt Charlotte had meticulously noted how many copies of this book she had sold. A large number. An astonishingly large number. Both the front and back of the form were filled with clusters of tally marks, and Valerie would have thought it a runaway bestseller if she hadn't noticed the date when the elderly bookseller first ordered the novel: 12/10/1959. 'Seems to be a long-term seller, at any rate,' she observed, replacing the card inside the book before closing it and putting it down. A cup of hot tea would be most welcome now. Valerie locked the door, took one of the chipped mugs from the cupboard above the sink, both of which were in a niche in the office and invisible from the shop, poured herself a finger's width of tea and filled the mug with water from the boiler. Sitting back down at the desk, she found a piece of paper and started jotting down some notes.

★ ★ ★

Business administration can be described as a science as useful as it is imprecise. It undoubtedly gives a grounding to a flighty young woman, as well as the necessary confidence — if this is naturally lacking — to regard even the most undoable tasks as doable, for example the management, rescue or even liquidation of a small bookshop whose owner has gone AWOL, to say nothing of the customers. And so it should come as no surprise that, at the end of a long evening, a to-do list with no fewer than eighty-four tasks lay beside the till, with the memorable heading, 'First Steps — Short-Term Measures', beneath which sat such important bullet points as: Cash Audit, Bank Appointment, Inventory, Materials Management, Check Deliveries and Payments, Overview of Cash Flow, Receivables, Accountant?, Overdraft Facility?, Account Balances, Results?

At this point in our story it is time to put the record straight about a widespread prejudice. Women in their mid-twenties, especially educated women and particularly those with glasses (although we should note here that Valerie was wearing contact lenses, at least on that day), are not necessarily interested in romance. On the contrary, they often tend to be marked by a pronounced sobriety, whose origin and aim are so uncertain that one must assume it has no particular significance. And anybody who had seen the young man knocking at the door around nine o'clock could not avoid coming to the same conclusion. Valerie opened the door and offered her cheek to Sven, while glancing up at the sky and wondering how much longer it would be before it began raining.

For his part, Sven, who had recently started as a trainee in a business consultancy, glanced into the shop, rolled his eyes and said by way of a greeting, 'I don't want to know what sort of money you've got to write off for the stock here.'

'Good point,' Valerie replied, hurrying back to the desk so she could jot down 'Inventory Valuation'. In truth, all manner of dead wood lurked on the shelves. It suddenly occurred to her that booksellers were apparently entitled to send books they'd ordered back to the publishers — 'remittances', as they were called. So she also added 'Remittances? Refunds/ Offsetting?' to her list.

'Are you finished?' Sven asked, as he stepped beside her and examined the desk.

Valerie looked up at him and noted that he was again trying to grow one of those ridiculous three-day beards. On day one his roundish face had a dirty tinge. It was scratchy, too, as she'd felt when they kissed each other. Tomorrow it would be really unpleasant, and the day after it would look awfully shabby.

'You ought to have a shave.'

'Hmm.'

'I'm almost done. Just let me do another security check.'

The inspection took precisely thirty seconds. The shop, barely more than forty square metres, the galley kitchen that doubled up as the office, perhaps ten, probably more like eight square metres: little space to patrol.

14

Valerie picked up her bag, thrust the Kafka novel in it, shoved Sven out of the shop and locked up behind her, without noticing the shadow that scurried past her feet.

3

Whoever declared May to be the 'merry month' must have lived on Mauritius. Or Hawaii. There wasn't much to be merry about in the climes of central Europe. Valerie's nascent cold had turned overnight into a full-blown infection. Ever since the previous evening, the sky had been practising for Armageddon. With clammy fingers Valerie jiggled the key into the lock, cursed because the door was stuck, threw herself against it, almost clattered to the floor, and was very glad finally to be inside. She left the dripping umbrella in a corner and fled to the loo, where she stared at a worn-out stranger in the tiny mirror above the small basin. The samovar, she remembered, grateful that Aunt Charlotte had been such an old-fashioned woman. That would come to her assistance now. She quickly filled the boiler, chucked a handful of tea into the pot and unwrapped her scarf to dry it over the back of the chair.

Ringelnatz & Co. had once been one of the most important, illustrious addresses in the neighbourhood. Established following those terribly dark years, from the outset the bookshop had been a beacon of culture, remaining so for many years as the young bookseller employed her wit and joie de vivre to seduce numerous young men into reading. Over time, however, circumstances had changed, the neighbourhood had changed. Of the two options — luxury redevelopment and gentrification, or decay and social decline — the neighbourhood that was home to Ringelnatz & Co. had been forced to take the latter. Accompanying this was the fact that the bookseller and her shop were both getting on in years. Sure, there was a phase in which she attracted sympathy merely on account of her presence, and even praise in the editorial sections of the free local papers. But this didn't gain her any readers, at least not any new ones. The old ones, those customers from years and decades past, remembered the shop and popped in again. They'd talk about the good old times, complain about how young people had no interest in books, buy themselves a first edition of a novel by Somerset Maugham ('For my granddaughter; I loved him when I was her age') and then disappear once more out of the elderly lady's life.

In spite of this, one had to concede that the bookshop — if one ignored a certain, albeit charming, shabbiness — was still a real gem, and not only on account of the floor-to-ceiling bookshelves made of huge, genuine walnut timbers, the splendid curtain or the excessively musical, but highly attractive floorboards, which — freshly waxed — recalled the polished planks of a luxury sailing boat. No, the chief appeal of the shop was, of course, its range of books, selected with as much intelligence and thoughtfulness as affection.

Valerie's intention had been to go home and make further notes to complete her to-do list, but she opted to read the rest of her Kafka novel and finally fell asleep on the sofa. When she woke up, she put the book on a stool, which the old lady must have used to reach books from higher shelves. She wouldn't be able to put it back; now it looked second hand. But, hold on, hadn't Valerie spotted a corner with antiquarian books on her inspection of the shop yesterday? Yes, she had. Taking a closer look, she noticed that a section of the shop, in fact the section furthest from the door (which didn't mean very much in such a small shop) was stocked with second-hand books. To be more accurate, many of them must have been third- or fourth-hand. Here were many tomes bound in leather with gold-embossed spines, some faded from years in the light, many well-thumbed. But all the volumes that Aunt Charlotte had collected in these two bookcases had quite clearly been handled with great care. Valerie picked out a book, which looked as if it must have been rebound at some point, and opened it — it looked like a collection of poems, but was in fact a novel:

You're about to read Italo Calvino's latest novel If on a Winter's Night a Traveller. *Relax. Compose yourself. Put every other thought aside. Let your surroundings blur into an indistinct haze. Better close the door; the television's always on in there. Tell the others right away, 'No, I don't want to watch telly!' Raise your voice or they won't hear you say, 'I'm reading! I don't want to be disturbed!' Maybe they haven't heard you, what with all that noise. Better say it even louder, shout out, 'I'm about to start Italo Calvino's new novel!' Or don't say it if you don't want to. Hopefully they'll leave you in peace.*

Valerie couldn't help smiling. She'd never come across an opening to a book like this.

Find the most comfortable position: sitting, stretched out, huddled or lying down. On your back, on your side, on

*your tummy. In an armchair, on the
sofa, on the rocking chair . . .*

Admittedly, it did all seem like a load of
nonsense — a highly dubious exercise in
silliness — but it was fun to read the
ever-surprising and confusing twists and
turns in the stories, from which a quite
unusual novel emerged, navigating Valerie
through eras and lands like a runaway literary
carrousel, shunning convention and conspir-
ing cheekily with the reader on every page.

And so our protagonist found herself in the
elderly bookseller's armchair once more, after
hours of enjoyable reading, while the samovar
boiled incessantly beside her, at the very least
giving off a pleasant warmth. She hadn't
drunk anything — she hadn't even poured a
cup — but she didn't care. On the contrary,
she discovered how good it felt to read a story
purely for its own sake. And to her complete
amazement she realized she enjoyed following
this peculiar author through the amusing
labyrinth of his finely crafted tales. It was
something she hadn't done since her
schooldays, when she'd regarded reading as a
particularly laborious form of mental torture.
Now at a distance, she recalled all the bizarre
things she'd had to learn: chiasmus and
tropes, pleonasm, metaphor, ellipsis and all

manner of other conceptual fog, behind which access to the written word was supposedly hidden. But this was certainly not the case with these stories. No, the more she thought in the writer's playful language, and the more intricately she became entangled in Italo Calvino's fascinating plot twists, the more fun she had, the more her curiosity grew.

Or, to put it in Calvino's words, *If you really think about it, I'm sure you'd find it preferable to have something in front of you and not know exactly what it is.*

★   ★   ★

One must imagine Ringelnatz & Co. to be a totally uncompetitive business by today's standards. Too little space. Only in exceptional cases could such a tiny shop be profitable — perhaps if it sold high-end goods such as jewellery and expensive watches, or exquisite cosmetics — and that's assuming a steady clientele that ages prosperously. But a bookshop will find it difficult to defy the dictates of the market. And even if we were to consider ourselves amongst the greatest optimists (which of course we do), in the world of small bookshops, Ringelnatz & Co. was really one of the smallest. A ground-level shop floor, its longer side faced the street, promoted by its large display window, divided in the middle by a glass door. Inside, floor-to-ceiling shelves were on both sides and at the back on the left, all tightly packed with books; at the back on the right a small staircase with two steps led up to the galley kitchen and two narrow doors — one to the lavatory, the other to the backyard, where any sort of social interaction had ceased long ago. All of this in barely fifty square metres.

In spite of the limited space, the old bookseller had managed to house an incredibly broad range of reading matter! Admittedly, there was no room for the books to show themselves off; customers were able to see the front covers of only a few. And yet, any passionate reader would find it hard to believe that they might fail to find the book of their choice in this treasury of literature. No lover of romantic tales, no reader of history books, no connoisseur of poetry . . . especially poetry! Valerie soon established that Aunt Charlotte must have had a weakness for poetry; it was very well represented among both the contemporary and antiquarian books. Whether it was the strictly rhyming and sometimes awkward verse of Andreas Gryphius or the nimble yet profound *Lieder* of Heinrich Heine, the elegiac sensuality of

Rilke, the brutal honesty of Trakl or the far-sighted dedication of Neruda — nothing was missing. Modern, comic, earthy. But there was a notable accent on humour, something for which the elderly bookseller seemed to be particularly fond.

After the Italo Calvino novel and two volumes of Robert Gernhardt, Valerie actually felt better! Literature as therapy? She'd never have subscribed to that. And yet, when two days later the young woman felt chirpy again and no longer found it a struggle to brace herself for the task in hand, she sensed that her small flights into realms of wit had helped her overcome her infection.

4

This may come as a surprise, but every now and then what appears self-evident is the last thing you notice. Valerie had spent more than two whole days in the old bookshop when it finally dawned on her that there was a void, something missing there which was urgently required. All of a sudden it was so obvious that she almost let out a quiet scream when she discovered it. Or rather didn't discover it. But then a number of things that had been veiled in a mild haze became crystal clear. With no computer there was no sensible system of stock control. And with no sensible system of stock control there was no sensible system at all — indeed, one would almost be forced to concede that there was no system whatsoever.

Except that this was not completely true. For Aunt Charlotte had certainly had a system. Only it was going to take Valerie more than just two days to get her head around the system in its entirety. Until that point, she would find herself shunted back into a pre-digital era, which in her case — she did belong, after all, to the generation of so-called

24

digital natives — could have also been called an antenatal era. At any rate, faced with this state of affairs she felt helpless.

She turned around and looked down from the small office into the shop. And there they stood. Thousands of them, without a single folder or file that might have given them some order, that might have sorted, managed, tamed them. They stood there, gazing back, and Valerie fancied she could almost feel them making fun of her. Books. Mountains of books. How had the old lady known what she had in stock? Or what she needed to order? Or whether it had already been ordered? Or whether it was still available or out of print? 'My God,' Valerie whispered, as she went down the two steps into the shop to wander along the shelves again and look once more at all the volumes with quite different eyes. A farm, yes, that was somewhere which she could imagine might still function without a computer. Or perhaps a greengrocer's, where they only sold a limited range of goods and it wasn't hard to keep an overview of such perishable stock — what they bought in the morning was sold by the evening. But with books, of which there were thousands, no, millions of different ones and which often stood on the shelves for weeks and months, maybe even years before they were finally sold . . . No, there had to be a system. It might be antediluvian, but there had to be some kind of functioning system.

Of course there was a system. It was bound up with index cards and catalogues as well as an array of binders that the elderly lady had put together over the years, and which her niece had until now simply failed to notice, just as you can look straight past an ancient and obsolete traffic sign by the roadside even though it's under your nose.

The index cards were in compartments in the two top drawers of the desk. Noted down in elegant yet painstaking handwriting were author, title, publisher, edition, price and order number, together with a variety of other rather opaque details. In tiny, but razor-sharp letters, the elderly lady had also made notes on the individual books. Points, as Valerie could see, with which she summarized the particular features of a book in a few words. Her curiosity aroused, she flicked through to the card for Calvino, Italo: *If on a Winter's Night a Traveller* and read, 'A bit frivolous, slightly whimsical, but wonderfully ironic — for those who don't (or shouldn't) take life so seriously.'

Could anybody else have put it better? Of course, this was exactly the point of that curious little volume. What about Kafka's

The Castle? To Valerie's disappointment her aunt hadn't made any notes on it. A quick glance at the other cards revealed that this was a rare exception. Why? Maybe there were books which were such must-reads that they didn't need any selling points. And perhaps *The Castle* was one of those.

As she gradually battled her way through the elderly lady's archive, Valerie realized there were a number of books that had been sorted without any keywords, such as Thomas Mann's *Buddenbrooks* or Charles Dickens's *Great Expectations*. Quite a few children's books fell into this category too. Beside *The Happy Leeward Isles* Aunt Charlotte had just put an exclamation mark. When Valerie went to get the book she discovered an extraordinarily long and jolly title: *The Journey of Captain Davorin Midrankovic and His Passengers to the Isle of Honey, the Isle of Peace, the Isle of Towers, the Isle Where the Fiddles Grow, the Isle of Brushes, the Isle of Gugelhupfs and the Isle of Beautiful Truth, Narrated by Himself and Written down by James Krüss for All Those Who Are Happy or Should Like to Be.*

Of course, before she could continue working it was essential for Valerie to read some lengthy passages from this enchanting book and actually feel a little happier. It was already early evening by the time she had got as far as a volume that bore the auspicious title: *A Very Special Year*, by . . . Intrigued, Valerie went to fetch this book from the shelves too (it stood between a Dorothy Parker biography and Ferdinand Pessoa's *The Book of Disquiet*) and sat down with it in the armchair, which had by now taken on the scent of her perfume (and of eucalyptus balm). The cover showed a ticket for passage on a ship, old-fashioned and appealing. And the moment she nipped open the book she was thrust straight into the middle of a story; it felt as if the text had whisked her away instantaneously.

There had been no forewarning of the sudden change in weather. To begin with it was barely more than a gentle breeze. The elegant silhouette of a woman of indeterminate age was reflected in the shop window. Her headscarf flew up in the wind. Julia turned around and was astonished to see that the wind, which had whipped up from nowhere, looked as if it might carry the woman off. She scuttled out into the street, vanishing for a moment in a group of people who crowded around her as quickly as they dispersed.

Just enough time for the stranger to undergo a wonderful transformation. The headscarf had disappeared, giving way to long, blonde hair that fluttered in the wind, while her dress was hidden beneath a light raincoat. As soon as the rain started, the woman opened a dark-blue umbrella that was so ordinary looking it almost rendered her invisible.

Julia had followed the stranger with her gaze without knowing why. And now, just as instinctively, she walked behind her, impervious to the wind and rain. The woman emanated a mysterious aura that held Julia spellbound. Totally oblivious to her surroundings, she guided her steps in the same direction the woman was heading. In spite of the sudden torrent, the stranger moved with a lightness as if she were not of this world. Fascinated, Julia came closer. They approached a small bridge, on the other side of which steps led up to the old town. As Julia walked onto the bridge a violent gust wrenched the woman's umbrella. Struggling to keep hold of it, the woman dropped her handbag. Then, in a single, fluid move-ment, she abandoned the umbrella that was spinning in the wind, picked up her bag and continued swiftly on her way. Julia watched the umbrella rise up into the sky then flap down into the river. Like a drowned butterfly, she thought. When she looked back the woman was gone.

Confused and slightly embarrassed, Julia stood on the bridge. How on earth did I end up here? she asked herself. What am I doing following this woman? By now she was drenched and starting to freeze. She would go back home and make a hot chocolate — yes, and quickly too, before she caught a cold. She had gone no more than a metre or two when, out of the corner of her eye, she noticed something glinting brightly: an envelope. She stopped to pick it up. It must have fallen out of the stranger's handbag. She looked over to the far side of the bridge and the steps, but the woman was nowhere to be seen. Julia stuffed the envelope in her pocket and scampered to a nearby porch, where she took it back out and examined it in the pale light of a gloomy, stormy afternoon. It bore no address or inscription. Only now did Julia realize that the envelope was not sealed. Opening the flap, she removed the contents: two train tickets that had remained passably dry. First class, she noted. They were for today. Two tickets to Paris.

Had the stranger been on her way to the station? Julia looked at her watch: just past six o'clock. The train left at half past seven. The route — over the bridge, up the steps and through the old town — was the right direction. But the elegant-looking stranger hadn't been carrying any luggage, had she? Would she have had to? No, she could have left it in a station locker to pick up prior to departure. In any event, she would need the tickets. Maybe every-thing would have turned out differently if the rain hadn't abated at that moment, to be superseded by the slant-ing, late-afternoon sun. But Julia took a decision that would change everything, not least — in fact this most of all — her whole life.

She hurried across the bridge, up the steps and through the old town. Half an hour later, she was at the station, where the train to Paris was already waiting.

The first-class carriage was at the end of the platform. But there was still enough time. Julia got on and made for the front of the train, carefully checking in every compartment to see whether the mysterious stranger was there. But she would be in the front carriage, obviously. Or should have been. For as it turned out the woman wasn't there either. She was nowhere to be seen. Maybe she'd arrived just before the train left. Julia checked the tickets to see whether a specific seat had been reserved for her. Seat 13. She was standing right next to it! Perfect, she could wait for the woman here. Sitting down, she gazed out of the window at the platform. From here she'd be able to see the stranger coming from far off.

But time passed and the departure drew irrevocably closer. Two tickets, Julia thought, there were two tickets in the woman's envelope — they must be for two seats next to each other. Julia glanced at them again: seat 13 and — seat 13. Puzzled, she looked at the numbers above the seats. Two tickets for seat 13? Impossible. And yet there it was on the ticket in black and white:

Carriage 12, Seat 13, both times. Until she realized what she'd completely failed to notice before: only the first ticket was for Paris. The second was from Paris to . . . At that moment she heard the guard's whistle. And in a fraction of a second she made a decision: she would travel. To Paris, and then on to

The text broke off in mid-sentence. Confused, Valerie turned the page. But on the next side and the one after that she found herself staring at blank paper. All the way to the final page the publication had turned into an empty book. The young woman put it down with a mixture of disappointment and fascination. How might the story continue? How would it end? The book was clearly a faulty copy. She picked up the card from Aunt Charlotte's archive again. Under publisher was a name she'd never heard of before: Millefeuille. She knew this as a cake, but as a publishing house . . . Still, the name seemed somehow appropriate: a thousand leaves. The index of publishers must be somewhere; Valerie had seen it the day before. When she finally found it she looked for 'Millefeuille'. But her intuition proved correct: 'Millefeuille' was not there. Now it might be the case, of course, that Millefeuille was just an imprint of a larger publishing house. But checking the publishing details at the front of the book didn't help, because there weren't any.

Author? Nothing. 'Who wrote this book, for goodness' sake?' Valerie wondered, opening the spine to check the blurb on the back cover, where she found the following meagre lines: *The author lives and works in Paris, Florence and St Petersburg. After a major unhappy love affair with a woman, he fell deeply and happily in love with literature, thereby discovering a new life. This book is dedicated to the mother of his three daughters.*

Hmm, Valerie thought. A trifle overblown and yet so damn little information. She shut the book and stroked the surface with her fingers. It was beautifully bound with an embossed title and even a ribbon marker in hopeful green. The work of an unknown author from an unknown publishing house, maybe a completely misprinted edition; who could say whether an error-free one existed? Nobody would ask for it, nobody would buy it and in this state it couldn't even be sold as a remainder at a bargain price. Valerie put it down, picked it up again and finally tossed it into a box already containing all sorts of pieces of paper that Valerie had no idea what to do with.

The curse of undertaking a spring clean is that to begin with the chaos multiplies massively. It's only when you get to the point of despair, when you're on the verge of either giving up or jumping out of the window, that the fog suddenly starts to lift as if by magic. Almost imperceptibly to begin with, but then in an increasingly triumphant fashion, a certain order is re-established, a lucidity emerges, which after all the stress and agony feels even more refreshing. Jumping out of the window wouldn't have got Valerie very far; the shop was on the ground floor, after all. Giving up wasn't part of her plan either, and generally wasn't an option amongst those with business degrees. But most importantly, she was far from the point of absolute chaos. Of course, Sven would have seen it differently. Which, indeed, he did when that day, or more precisely that evening after work — which for trainee management consultants means some time comfortably after nine o'clock — he knocked on the shop window and waited for Valerie to let him out of the biting cold and into the warmth.

'Should I be worried?' Sven asked, taking off his coat and throwing it into a corner. 'You're working longer hours than me.'

'No idea. I mean, you should always look at things from the end point. But, to be honest, I can't see an end,' Valerie sighed, rubbing her eyes. Had she actually eaten anything today? She couldn't remember. Probably not since breakfast, and that had been a white coffee and a bowl of muesli. No surprise, then, that she felt giddy.

'Sit down, I shan't be much longer.'

'OK.' Sven sank into the armchair and leaned his head back. He took out his smartphone to check emails and scroll through the news. 'Shit,' he cursed. 'No juice. Have you . . . ?' But then he remembered that Valerie had a different phone and he couldn't charge his with her adaptor. As for the elderly bookseller, it wasn't even worth asking; she'd been way behind the times. He put his smartphone on the small table where a pile of books stood, and studied the spines of the diverse volumes.

'The *Kamasutra*?' he said finally with a mixture of amusement and approval. 'Don't tell me your aunt sold erotic literature here too.'

'What?'

'There's a *Kamasutra* here between Schiller and Schnitzler.'

'Oh yes, right.' Valerie looked up from her list. 'She had a system and I'm in the process of sifting out the most important books from it. That's my first result.'

But Sven wasn't really listening. He'd slid out the book and started studying it. Perhaps Valerie had carried on talking, but if so he wasn't aware of it. The truth is that literature can grab hold of us and capture our entire attention. It can transport us to other worlds, free us from our everyday cares. We can lose ourselves in literature. Even terribly prosaic individuals are receptive to this, providing it's the right book. Which was clearly the case with Sven and the *Kamasutra*. Valerie had just switched off the desk lamp and packed up her bag when her boyfriend laughed out loud. 'You've got to see this!' he giggled.

Now it was Valerie's turn to lean her head back. 'What?'

'They were quite weird, those ancient Indians.'

'There are ancient Egyptians and ancient Romans. I've also heard of ancient Persians, but ancient Indians? I think they're still the same people . . . '

'So what, look at this!' he said, resting the book on his lap. The colour in his face indicated that he was nowhere near as exhausted as Valerie. She stood next to him and bent over.

'So?'

'That's impossible in real life,' Sven

laughed. 'Just a completely weird sex fantasy.'

'Well, as far as I know this is a scientific book of sorts. I presume that everything in there *is* possible.' She took a closer look. 'Having said that . . . '

Perhaps it was the slight dizziness that had taken hold of her, perhaps the vague awareness that Sven was breathing more rapidly. Perhaps it was the dim glow from this one reading lamp that bathed the entire shop in a very modest light. Anyway, Valerie perched on the soft arm of the chair, leaned back on her Sven, grabbed the book, leafed through a couple of pages, muttered, 'We really ought to try that out sometime,' felt her breathing getting faster too, turned off the light, put the book down and her hand back to where it had just been resting. Sven took a deep breath, turned the light back on and got up.

'Great curtain,' he said in a slightly hoarse voice, undoing the cord that tied back the large stage curtain behind the shop window. 'And a great chair.'

'Reading chair,' Valerie specified.

'Let's do some studying then.'

★　★　★

What a marvellous invention stage curtains are. Devised to hide the banal and whet our

38

appetite for the extraordinary. They create the space for our imagination by eliminating the external perspective. Stage curtains embed our attention in the necessary mixture of mystery and anticipation. In a sense one could argue that there is a performance on either side of the stage curtain in Ringelnatz & Co. The main characters introduce themselves in the proscenium — selected titles which, thanks to their topicality, their particularly charming features or because the elderly bookseller held them in great esteem, are like lighthouses attracting the curiosity of passers-by. To the rear of the stage, the entire mass of players, utterly inconceivable in their diversity, so overwhelming that each one of them can become for the spectator the lead protagonist. Each book an event, turned into a theatrical production solely thanks to this heavy, deep-red curtain with its golden tassled edging, as old-fashioned as it is voluptuous, which was not pulled back again until the following morning to free up the view to an interested observer: Valerie, who until now hadn't given it a glance. She stood inside the small bookshop, somewhat dishevelled from a largely sleep-deprived night full of various *Kamasutra*-related studies, but pleasantly exhausted, and she realized to her astonishment that this most important PR tool for Ringelnatz & Co. had till now completely escaped her attention.

Well, over the course of the day she would subject the books to careful scrutiny. To start with she pulled out a handful and, obeying a spontaneous hunch, put the *Kamasutra* in one of the spaces that had become free. Then she left the shop with her boyfriend to get something to eat finally.

5

A cabinet of fantasies, a source of knowledge, a collection of lore from past and present, a place to dream . . . A bookshop can be so many things. Of course, on a very banal level it is also a store of printed matter to be sold to customers. But anyone who engages with the diversity a bookshop offers can experience epiphanies of a quite different and exceptionally sensual nature!

It was a well-thumbed little book, wrapped in grey-black paper, one of those works so easy to overlook in a superficial review of the stock. Most of the gold embossing on the spine had disappeared due to a tear in the binding. Valerie didn't examine it closely; she just pulled out the book to note down the author and title. Both were set between two small stars, also embossed in gold, on a very beautiful oxblood vignette on the front cover: Gustav Flaubert, *Memoirs of a Madman*. And while she wondered why this name hadn't been written with an 'e' — Gustave Flaubert — she opened the book and discovered that inside, that's to say on the title page, it had been printed in two colours:

red and black on white. In the bottom right-hand corner on this first page (something seemed to be missing; maybe the book had once had a frontis-piece) was an illegible name and a year: '39'. As a note on the very last page said, this edition had appeared in 1922. The book smelled faintly of printer's ink and pipe smoke. How many hands might this have passed through before ending up amongst the antiquarian books in the shop? And who had brought it here?

The text was sharply printed and — as Valerie noted when she ran her fingers across the pages — slightly debossed. On those pages with only a few lines of text, the imprint of the type on the reverse side was clearly visible. At the bottom of page 17 there was a tiny annotation, set apart from the main text: '2 Flaubert'. She found a similar annotation on page 33: '3 Flaubert'. The book came to an end shortly after '7 Flaubert'; it only had 99 pages in total. But, as Valerie worked out, each annotation marked a so-called printed sheet, which consisted of sixteen pages. In vain she tried to picture the specific technique by which one of these sheets would have to be folded, printed and cut to end up with a meaningful sequence of text, or rather the only correct sequence, the desired sequence, the tale of a young Flaubert or another of the countless stories that had made it into book form over the past five hundred years.

The Flaubert book was neither one of the most beautiful nor best-smelling on the shelves. Not even the works of Ringelnatz, all of them fairly conventional-looking tomes (scarcely daring to emphasize the originality of the ideas they harboured), belonged in this category. But there were myriad books whose aesthetic charm was irresistible, so long as you gave it the opportunity to work its magic. The editions of Heinrich Heine, for example, which in just two volumes of delicate lightweight paper managed to reproduce all the fragility of Heine's divine and wicked poetical art. You handled each page with the greatest respect, allowing the airy, shimmering ideas to take effect. There was the cloth-bound Balzac, whose dignified under-statement was the very opposite of the pompous man himself — a commercial writer of the highest calibre — but it did lend the work a more universal validity. Although the volume was almost odourless, it had a flawlessly stitched binding that shimmered impishly. The ostentatious Dostoevsky, bound entirely in cognac-coloured leather that smelled slightly like an old, long-distance train compartment, in which a delegation of well-off gentlemen discuss prices on the wood market. On the front cover, embossed deeply in gold, was the author's signature with its bold loops that rose as high as they sunk low, but completely illegible; it could have easily been the signature of any old vet. A perfidious edition of Christian Morgenstern's *Gallows Songs*, which may have lain for goodness knows how long on the bedside table of a fashionable young lady — no, more likely under her pillow. The scent of her perfume had penetrated deeply into the rather brittle and yellowed paper, which was of the plainest quality and had already torn in places. The book's appearance stood in sharp contrast to its olfactory charms, which made it interesting. Valerie was so curious that she sat down to investigate further. After spending a while getting used to the author's bizarrely crafted ideas, she came across a poem entitled *The Daynight Lamp*. And as she was reading it, something switched on in her mind:

> *Korf invents a daynight lamp*
> *that turns the brightest day*
> *into darkest night*
> *the moment you flick the switch.*
>
> *When in Congress, by the ramp*
> *he demonstrates his light.*

All who know their stuff, they
must face up to the fact, which —

(Darkness replaces the light of day,
applause in the House reaches fever pitch)
(They cry to the butler, Herr Hamp:
'Turn on the lights') — must face up
to the fact, which

is that this very lamp
does indeed turn the brightest day
into darkest night
when you flick the switch.

Valerie stood up, put the book down, turned out the lights and inhaled deeply the discoveries in this wonderful cabinet of dreams, the scents of all the new and old books, the aroma of their experiences and promises, their curses and prophesies, of the hands in which they had rested, the care with which the paper manufacturer, printer and binder had worked on them, the ink with which they were printed, the glue, the cloth, the leather, the covers and dust-jackets, the stitching, the ribbons and tissue paper. No perfumery could produce as perfect a blend from the interplay of countless aromas as a bookshop, in which old and new works were arranged with love. As *The Daynight Lamp* proved, if for a moment you can stop regarding a book as purely a means of conveying ideas, it is an utterly sensual experience — a work of total art.

*   *   *

It's not particularly difficult to run a bookshop successfully, Valerie thought. You need the most basic principles of management, a sensible business plan, a little negotiating skill, a few contacts and a large helping of magic. Of course, not everyone who sails through time and space with a bookshop can master the last of these. Nor could Valerie. She didn't even come close, she would soon realize. For you could check, correct, predict all the figures; you could count, order and make an inventory of all the books. You could work from early in the morning to late in the evening and even at night. But if you couldn't perform magic then all this was in vain. It felt as if there must be a million books available. Perhaps there were many more than this. Different titles! And several editions of many of these. Who could ever know what from all this material would really interest the reader? Who could even begin to make a selection from this inconceivable mass of books that had accumulated over hundreds of years? Didn't managing a product range mean that you had to know everything to be able to sift out what you could recommend to your readers? But perhaps the bookshop itself was a work, too: an anthology of other works that comprised its soul. Wasn't every shop inevitably the expression of its owner's individuality? Nobody could know a million books.

Limits were essential, therefore. Every bookseller selected from what they knew and liked. This gave the bookshop its own personality. Then there were orders from customers who asked for certain books they couldn't find among the stock. If this happened frequently, the bookseller would buy copies of the title to have it in stock for when the next customer came asking for it. And that's how a bookshop evolved, like a child that grows up, severing the umbilical cord from its parents and developing its own character, its distinct personality: unpredictable, idiosyncratic and full of surprises. But the more strongly this character is developed, the more strength and empathy it needs to master it and show off its best. It's like a hot-blooded horse that needs a first-rate rider.

Valerie, however, was not a particularly good rider. To tell the truth, she wasn't a rider at all. In actual fact, she had the feeling, even after just a few weeks, that she was the one being ridden here. If she trotted in one direction (for example by drawing up a new price list) the strange world of bookselling would mercilessly rein her in (because prices are fixed by the publisher long before the product is in the shops). If she galloped in the opposite direction (let's say by means of bold discounting to gain greater support from publishing partners) the law would force her to make a U-turn (in this case because discounts in Germany are only allowed up to a certain level; anything beyond this is termed 'unfair competition'). The combination of stipulations, conventions, customs, regulations, and therefore opportunities, appeared such a complex amalgam that big leaps seemed out of bounds from the beginning. It was only with content that there were no limits and this lack of limits was so absolute that, in addition to the aforementioned qualities needed for the felicitous management of a successful bookshop, Valerie soon stumbled upon the final, equally indispensable, requirement: unqualified madness.

★ ★ ★

Experienced readers of novels that deal with booksellers may at this juncture argue that another fixed element is essential for everything to run smoothly: a mysterious female cat that was either a pharaoh or temple dancer in a previous life, or alternatively an unscrupulously gallant torn with differently coloured eyes and a missing claw. In fact Ringelnatz & Co. had the necessary technical provision for this: a window onto the backyard, tall and narrow (both the window and the yard). When Valerie opened it for some oxygen to combat the tiredness that had overcome her, she thought she glimpsed a modest grey tabby darting away beneath the sill. The yard looked like the set for a Mafia film. In one corner raindrops tussled with brown leaves, while the wind cut so bitterly through the ramshackle walls that Valerie decided it would be better to tilt the window open from the top to stop it from slamming shut in her face. Beforehand, though, she placed a saucer of milk on the sill. Then she lay in wait, wondering what name she'd give the cat. 'Ruby' came to mind, but that didn't suit grey. 'Grisella'! But wasn't that the name of a little donkey from a children's story she vaguely remembered? 'Grisaille', perhaps? Valerie didn't know that this was a painting technique for oil designs. So Grisaille it stayed. She thought it sounded like a friendly old lady, such as Aunt Charlotte. She kept thinking about this until the cat popped onto the window sill and turned out not to be a cat after all. Not even a torn cat. Grisaille was another beast altogether and, yes, Valerie got quite a shock when there it was staring straight at her just a few inches away, albeit separated by the windowpane. For Grisaille was almost the opposite of a cat: she was a rat.

6

It was some time before Valerie finally secured an appointment with the bank. Till then she'd just had a statement in the post for the end of the quarter. As was to be expected, she saw that there hadn't been any payments in and only a few deductions — mainly from the bank. Account charges, debit interest, postage, transaction fees. Money for nothing. One ought to be a bank, Valerie thought, as she got on her bicycle and rode to the branch where Aunt Charlotte had her account. She'd packed all the lists that she'd made in the previous weeks: debit, credit, stock, outstanding receivables etc. Now she had to find out what dark spots were still lurking in the finances.

The customer account manager greeted her with an engaging smile and a glance at her cleavage. As she followed him to one of the consultation booths that had been set up for discreet conversations to the rear of the service centre, she fastened another button on her blouse.

'Right, we're very pleased you've come to see us. How is your . . . ' — he looked at the letter she'd written him, which was now in a folder — 'aunt?'

'Thanks for asking,' replied Valerie, who over the course of her studies had learned when it was better to keep some pieces of information to yourself. 'She's fine.'

'I assume you have a letter giving you power of attorney?'

'Of course.'

From her documents Valerie took a sheet of paper on which she'd knocked out the following using Aunt Charlotte's old typewriter: *I hereby give my niece Valerie D. the power of attorney to look after my bank affairs. Yours faithfully, Charlotte K.* She'd extravagantly covered the squiggle beneath this with the freshly inked Ringelnatz & Co. stamp. The banker took the scrap of paper without affording it more than a cursory glance and slipped it into his folder.

'Now,' he said, trying to sound businesslike as he noticed to his chagrin the fastened button, 'what brings you here?'

'We're in the process of giving Ringelnatz & Co. a thorough overhaul to relaunch the company. Now that we've finished our assessment of stock and have checked and recorded all the bookkeeping matters, assets, liabilities etc., it's time to address the company's cashflow and financial resources. We're also subjecting to scrutiny our lines of credit and the terms of our business transactions.'

The account manager's gaze had wandered upwards in slight disbelief and settled on her eyes. It took him a moment to switch from 'petty nuisance' to 'business meeting'. Clearing his throat, he leafed briefly through what was a very thin folder and said, 'Well, I'm afraid we can't really talk of cash*flow* in relation to your . . . business.' He scratched his neck. 'For some time now it's been more like a standstill.'

'Obviously, the amount of cashflow we generate is directly linked to how the business is running — and to which bank account we're using.'

'Yes, of course,' the banker hurried to agree, but then paused. 'Hold on, are you saying there are other banks?'

'Of course,' Valerie bluffed. 'No healthy company would shackle itself to just one credit institution, would it?'

'Well, you shouldn't look at it that way,' the man contradicted her. She bet his hair had already started thinning at school and now, on the cusp of middle age, he was probably wondering what he was doing still sitting in this cubbyhole, haggling with the most minor businesses over the most minor conditions, while colleagues of his were playing at being financial jugglers in the skyscrapers of the bank's headquarters and were allowed to gamble with billions. 'I mean, a bank isn't just responsible for transactions; it can be a long-term partner for your business. We see ourselves, at least, as a universal adviser for all financial questions. Look, with our financial products and services — '

Valerie cut him off with a wave of her hand. 'First I'd like to see what liabilities we have and what the interest rate is.'

The adviser flicked through the file again. Then he rocked his head from side to side and said, 'Your bookshop did have a business overdraft facility on its current account . . . '

'Did have?'

'Hmm, yes, well at some point it was converted into a private overdraft facility.' He cleared his throat again.

'At some point?'

'Two years ago, to be precise.'

'For what reason?'

'Errm . . . I'm afraid I can't see that from the documents in front of me,' the man said. His uncertainty made it blatantly clear that the bank had taken her aunt for a ride.

'Are there other documents, then?'

'Well, I don't know of any . . . '

'Then I presume that the bank did it purely out of its own interests and without any prior consultation with my aunt.'

'But we did write to her. Look . . . ' He pointed to a standard letter with the bank's letterhead.

'And did you get a reply?'

'Hmm . . . no, clearly not.'

'Well then, as you I'm sure know, your unilateral action is not legally binding. I'd like to object to the change, and demand a recession and recalculation based on the value from that date.'

'I don't know if I can do that without consulting my manager . . . '

'Both of us know that not only can you do that, you *must* do it,' Valerie asserted, bending over the table. 'Let's move onto the debts.'

'Debts?'

'How high are the liabilities that Ringelnatz & Co. currently have with your bank?'

'Oh.' The adviser essayed a smile but it looked forced. 'Well, you'll be pleased to hear that there aren't any liabilities, apart from the negative balance on the last statement.'

He adjusted his glasses, looked at the statement as if it were an imperial proclamation and said, 'Five euros eighteen.' He cleared his throat again. 'I should point out, however, that your aunt's private wealth is almost all gone. She won't be able to inject capital for much longer. I mean, as she's done over the past few years.'

Valerie shrugged, seemingly casually, but inwardly at a loss. 'She won't have to inject any more capital,' she curtly informed the dumbfounded banker. Giving him a nod, she stood up.

★　★　★

To Valerie's astonishment she found out over the coming days that, although there were pretty much zero cash reserves in the small business that was Ringelnatz & Co., Aunt Charlotte had nonetheless carefully avoided accruing anything like debts. Whenever a financial hole had appeared, she'd plugged it with her own money — during all those years she'd run the shop she gradually returned to the business the little money she'd been able to save. There weren't any other banks of course, nor any other assets — but there weren't other liabilities elsewhere either.

Basically, the appointment with the accounts manager had been totally unnecessary. His involvement extended to little more than passing on a statement of net income (although it had been years since one could talk of net income) and an invoice for his work.

The only real items in Aunt Charlotte's

business accounts were the quarterly direct debits for gas, electricity and water, as well as the incidental costs for the premises. What Valerie hunted for unsuccessfully was a regular rent payment, until finally she discovered that the elderly bookseller actually owned the shop! The business itself might not have been thriving, but Aunt Charlotte had had money in bricks and mortar! Or she still did. For in spite of all the conclusive proof Valerie was faced with, she didn't want to exclude the possibility that the old lady might still be alive. Hopefully she was. Valerie wished it to be true. But of course she was enough of a realist to know how low the probability was.

★ ★ ★

'The appointment was a roaring success, by the way!' she later told her new friend, who was now showing up on a daily basis, over a saucer of milk. 'Bankers are as predictable as an atomic clock.' Valerie sipped her tea and watched Grisaille's pretty pink tongue lap away at the white liquid. If you set aside your prejudices and look at a rat close up, you can't help finding it beautiful. Rats have coats that shine like silk, clever, alert eyes, while their claws are tiny masterpieces of evolution.

What's more, Grisaille always had one ear open for Valerie's reflections. And now Valerie even dared leave the window open when the rat emerged from its obscure corner.

In spite of this proximity to literature, however, Grisaille was more interested in her own tail than the tales housed in the bookshop. When Valerie once tried to read her a few lines of Susanna Clarke's *The Ladies of Grace Adieu*, the beast fled — which can't have had anything to do with Clarke. At least this cleared up what species of rat Grisaille belonged to. Valerie thought that it couldn't be *Rattus norvegicus*, the common sewer rat, or *Rattus rattus*, the established house rat, but *Rattus alliterarius* and thus a welcome distraction from the insularity that usually envelops the written word and its reader. With this, Valerie added a sixty-seventh species of rat to the sixty-six already recognized by zoology.

'Do you think Aunt Charlotte is still alive?'

Grisaille looked at her with her pitch-black, reflective eyes. Was she smiling?

'Thanks,' Valerie said after a while. 'I bet you're right. She's travelling somewhere in the history of the world. Maybe she hijacked an underground train and absconded to South America with it. Or right now she's inviting a few Eskimos to share an excellent bottle of Tunisian vodka.'

Grisaille smirked, then lapped up a little more milk. When Valerie poured herself some more tea the rat vanished. But then the bell by the door rang and the postwoman came in.

'You're not going to believe this,' she said by way of a greeting, handing Valerie the usual bundle of bills, flyers and a trade journal that Valerie had never even glanced at. But right at the top was a postcard. An idyllic scene with a sea view that invited envy. At the top was written 'Porto'.

Curious, Valerie turned over the card and read:

Dear Valerie,
I hope all's well with you. Please don't
be worried about me! Bye bye!
Charlotte

It seemed to Valerie as if she were looking straight through these barren lines at Grisaille's mysterious little rat smile.

★   ★   ★

The card from Portugal remained the only sign of life from the old woman. Days, weeks and months passed, but the postwoman never arrived again with anything similar. Instead Valerie felt herself being dragged more deeply into an existence that was quite alien to her. She wasn't a bookseller, she wasn't the old lady from Ringelnatz & Co. She wasn't even a big reader, not at all. And yet these days she kept catching herself, as if by coincidence, with books in her hands, immersed in stories and poems. She sorted, analysed, did the accounts, she drank the elderly bookseller's tea, sat in her armchair, pored over her business documents. And she chatted to rats. While Aunt Charlotte was drifting heaven knew where, Valerie was gradually taking her place. And she was alarmed to note that she felt increasingly comfortable doing so.

7

Anybody who imagines there are no surprises to be had in a bookshop is quite mistaken. It is true that bookselling might be regarded as predictable and even a little boring from an entrepreneurial perspective. But not everything is foreseeable. No, however rare it is, the unexpected inevitably comes into play: the customer.

When the bell rang, which had hung over the door from the time the shop was founded, Valerie's initial reaction was to look at her mobile. Not that her ringtone sounded remotely similar. But if anything happened these days, it usually happened via a digital link to the outside world. She'd just been staring at a list which her aunt had entitled, surprisingly, 'Outstanding Items', but which contained nothing of the sort that a business graduate might consider to be 'outstanding items' — much more a sort of incoherent to-do list, which also included a few details of books still in storage, though Valerie hadn't looked at it that closely yet.

The young man stood quite unexpectedly in the doorway, favourably lit by the mild glow of an early summer evening. 'Are you still open?' he asked diffidently.

'Are we still open?' Valerie repeated, slightly confused. In fact she'd arranged to meet a couple of friends at the cinema and ought to have left long ago. 'Actually we're not,' she said hesitantly. The film was starting in half an hour, and these friends had already been teasing her for never being around any more.

'Oh, I'm very sorry to have disturbed you then,' the young man mumbled, turning to go.

On the other hand, the shop's sums were not so great that she could afford not to give them a boost using every means at her disposal.

'But we'll happily make an exception for you,' exclaimed Valerie, who really couldn't justify losing a potential sale. She rushed around the desk and down the steps to the shop floor. Why do I keep saying 'we'? she wondered. Is there anybody else here responsible for this shop? Thousands of books stared at her and Valerie looked at the floor, inwardly ashamed. Outwardly, she smiled at the customer, who was wearing an elegant, if somewhat old-fashioned between-seasons coat, from the pocket of which the headlines of the *Frankfurter Allgemeine Zeitung* poked out nosily; a rather creased shirt, with spectacles in the breast pocket; and

Italian shoes, which may no longer have been brand new, but were well looked after. 'What are you looking for?'

'Do you mind if I have a quick look around?'

Valerie was not sure, but she thought she heard a faint accent in his voice, a tone which sounded foreign and charming. 'Of course,' she said. 'Please feel at home.'

'That's an invitation I don't have to be offered twice in a bookshop, especially not in one arranged so marvellously as this!' The young man had the eye of a connoisseur, which ploughed along the rows of shelves, glinting each time it stopped at a particular volume. From time to time his gaze slipped and brushed the young bookseller as if by chance. Valerie pretended unsuccessfully to look as if she had urgent things to do behind his back. There was something about him, something you rarely saw — he radiated a distinguished sophistication. Sven could have taken a leaf out of his book.

Where are you from? Valerie wondered, with a furtive smile at the strange contradiction of his completely untamed hair and carefully picked elegant wardrobe. His shoes gleamed, his snow-white cuffs protruded exactly a finger's width from his sleeves, as if he were applying to be a concierge at a grand hotel or accepted in an English club, and yet with his shock of hair, beard and melancholy eyes he looked like a communist revolutionary. Valerie couldn't help finding him exceedingly interesting. Maybe even more than interesting . . . To still be standing after the looks she'd been firing at him he must be made of wood or stone.

★　★　★

It had been the elderly lady's great talent, which she'd honed and perfected over all the years she'd spent as a bookseller, that she'd possessed an almost magical sense for finding and stocking the right books. The 'right books' always meant those that the customers entering her shop really wanted to read. Although it wasn't always the case that these customers knew this beforehand. On the contrary, they'd often come in just 'to have a look around'. But then they'd go away with one or several books that would often change their lives.

Anybody entering Ringelnatz & Co. was subjected to a rigorous examination by the elderly bookseller's dependable eye. Sometimes a short conversation helped, sometimes watching how potential customers went along the shelves showed her what would be suited to them. Often a customer would pick the wrong book, upon which the elderly lady would find ways and words to dissuade them, for nothing is more dangerous for people's reading pleasure and thus for booksellers than the wrong book at the wrong time. With a sure hand she would take out another tome, open it as if at random, appear to read a short passage or two, then look up in astonishment and say, 'You really ought to see this.' Or she would assume her legendary mischievous smile and raise a finger, as if urgently needing to disclose a secret, before saying, 'An excellent choice. But I'm sure you don't know this book yet!' And as if by magic she'd whip out a volume tailor-made for the customer, and which would bring them inspiration, insight or simply a great deal of pleasure.

★ ★ ★

Valerie, of course, possessed no such bookselling magic. She wouldn't have known what advice to give — negative or positive — if a customer had asked her. But the young man didn't ask. Rather he kept browsing the stock in a knowledgeable yet modest way, regularly plucking a book from the shelves, opening it, stroking the pages with his slender fingers (instinctively Valerie checked to see whether he wore a ring, which he didn't), while a delicate smile appeared on his lips. At one point Valerie glimpsed a critical frown on his brow.

'Have you been here before?' she heard herself ask.

'In your bookshop you mean? No, I'm afraid not. But I could spend my life here.'

With an embarrassed smile Valerie withdrew. 'If there's anything I can do for you . . . ' she muttered, before sitting back at the desk in the office, not without continuing to watch the strange visitor through the door. Spend my life here, she thought, and realized that she could very well imagine that. But after a while she got back down to her tasks, leafing through the publishing catalogues that had arrived in the post, and trying to ignore the peculiar disturbance that the young man's arrival had caused.

When she turned her attention to him again it was dark outside. Valerie looked at her watch. She cleared her throat. 'I don't wish to sound impolite . . . ' she said, going down the two steps to the shop floor with the keys in her hand.

'Oh, I must apologize, it's me who's been impolite,' the young man hurried to say. 'I've detained you. You were meant to close ages ago, weren't you? I'm terribly sorry; I completely forgot the time.'

'Didn't you find anything?' Valerie asked. She felt that after hours of reading for free in her bookshop he really could buy something.

'Too much!' the man replied, brushing away a strand of his thick hair from his forehead. 'I'd love to take the whole lot.'

'Perhaps you ought to start with just one or two,' Valerie suggested.

'You're right. Absolutely right.' Slowly he turned 360 degrees, as if waiting for one of the books to jump out at him to buy. Then he took a few steps to the rear of the shop and laid his hands on a second-hand volume. It wasn't anything special; Valerie hadn't noticed the book before. On the slightly yellowed jacket was a detail from a painting, perhaps from the art nouveau era: A.S. Byatt, *Possession*.

'Do you know it?' the young man asked. His eyes blazed at hers.

'Ermm . . . no. To be honest, it's the first time I've seen it.'

'Oh. You should read it.' He passed it to her. 'Choose any page.'

Any page. Valerie opened it. Page 186–87. 'So?' she said. 'What now?'

'May I?' He took the book back and his voice became very soft when he said, 'It's a light novel. But it's told in the way stories ought to be told.'

'And how's that?' Valerie asked, half out of amusement, half out of curiosity.

'With joy in the magic of words.' And he read out loud: 'Silky snow, pomegranates, drugget, yellowish, breastplate, gas-mantels, metal covers . . . Or here, later on: shuttle, Peephole, patient, generous, Noah's ravens, Swammerdam, sense, grosser . . . and then: spilt milk, Melusine myth, Vestal Lights . . . Isn't that wonderful? This cornucopia of possibilities of giving expression to a story?'

Valerie couldn't suppress a smile. 'Yes, you're right,' she said. 'It is a particular type of magic.'

'You said it.' He offered her a smile, which took her breath away momentarily. 'I'd love to take it.'

'Of course,' she said, swallowing. She held out her hand and felt his fingers touch hers as he passed her the book. Her heart missed a beat . . . No, that would be one cliché too many. Even if that's exactly how it felt to Valerie. We can state here that she'd slightly fallen in love with this unknown, attractive and cultivated young man.

'That's . . . ' She turned the book over and looked in vain for a price label. 'Well . . . ' She examined the first page, then the last. 'It's second-hand.'

'And in excellent condition. Would you be

happy with, let's say, a hundred euros? I mean, it *is* signed by the author.'

'That's true,' Valerie said. 'But I reckon a hundred euros is rather too much than too little.'

'Are you just helping out here?' the young man asked, taking out a worn brown wallet, from which he plucked a brand-new note to give her. It was so immaculate it almost looked like a forgery.

'Not really,' Valerie explained, hesitating only briefly to take the money. 'The shop belongs to my aunt. She's disappeared and I'm trying to sort out the chaos she left behind.' She shrugged and climbed the two steps up to the till. 'It's a complicated story.'

'I like complicated stories,' the young man said, following her. When Valerie turned to him he was standing so close that the two of them almost bumped into each other.

'Sorry,' he said.

'No worries. Do you need a receipt?'

'No.' In one perfectly elegant movement he thrust the book into the inside pocket of his coat and was about to leave with a small bow when he suddenly stopped and stared at the floor, no, not at the floor, but at the recycling bin. Or rather, inside the recycling bin.

'You've got *A Very Special Year*?'

'Pardon? Oh, well, hmmm, I'm afraid it's a

. . . it was a defective copy.'

'A defective copy?' As delicately as he could, the young man took the book from the pile of paper, opened it and said, 'There had been no forewarning of the sudden change in weather.' Visibly moved, he looked up. 'Will you sell it to me?'

'Listen,' Valerie tried to explain, 'this book is completely misprinted. The text breaks off after a few pages.' She shrugged apologetically.

'Oh, I see,' the young man said, giving her a puzzled look. 'You don't want to give it away?'

'No, I do. Please, please take it,' Valerie said. 'Have it as a present.'

'A . . . present? I . . . I can't accept that. You don't know how long I've been looking for this book.'

'And then all you find is a defective copy.' Valerie smiled with a mixture of sympathy and amusement. But the young man laughed as if he'd cracked a brilliant joke, before thanking her again with radiant eyes, pocketing this book too and vanishing into the darkness. Valerie remained at the door of the little bookshop for a short while, watching him go, although in the gloom of the ancient street lighting she wasn't sure she could see exactly where he was. Then she felt a gust of wind drive down the street, bringing with it such an unexpected downpour that she had to take refuge inside. As she slammed the door behind her she repeated the words the stranger had muttered only a few minutes earlier: 'There had been no forewarning of the sudden change in weather.'

8

Another of the elderly bookseller's whims had been to keep letters from customers who'd written after reading particular books. She'd filed them away in what was now an overflowing folder. It had been some time, a few years in fact, since Aunt Charlotte had received her last letter; at least, the last one she'd filed was dated the same year that Valerie had finished school. Sven had taken the folder and was browsing through it, while Valerie went through the inventory, recording every single book — she had just got to shelf thirteen. 'Or this one!' he cried, citing another example: '*I really couldn't see anything coming in this novel! It's a masterpiece! You gave me a sleepless night! Thanks!* God, she's hysterical that one. Can't write a sentence without shoving an exclamation mark at the end. *This book is a revelation! How come so few people know it?*'

'Does she say what book it is?'

'Yes, wait a moment, it's somewhere in the letter.' He made that pointless and embarrassing dum-da-dum-da-dum-da-dum sound, which some people do when they're reading to signal to other people that they're doing what they're purporting to do: reading. It's a well-honed insecurity they like to round off with an 'Ah'. 'Ah, here,' Sven said. '*By Night Under the Stone Bridge*. By . . . '

'Leo Perutz.'

'Not bad. We ought to put you up for a quiz show.'

'Wasn't too hard. I just had the book in my hand.'

'If it's such a revelation, maybe you ought to read it,' Sven said off-handedly, without any attempt to sound serious about his suggestion. But even as he was reading out the title, Valerie took hold of the book again. It was an old edition, not an antiquarian one, but with a slightly faded spine and yellowed pages. She'd immediately taken to the title; it sounded mysterious and enticing.

'Or this one here!' Sven called out. He was holding another letter: '*Once again you found something exactly to my taste. And yet the books you recommend me are all so different that I'm at a loss as to how I end up liking them all so much. Thank you very much! Yours, Natalia de Bon-Leclerq.* Lovely writing paper — looks like it's from the nineteenth century. A marquise. Natalia Marquise de Bon-Leclerq du Tour. Unbelievable. How come the shop's in the red if your aunt had customers like that?'

'That's something I'd love to know too,' Valerie replied, brushing a hair from her face. Yes, it did irritate her that Sven sat around either fiddling with his smartphone and cracking stupid jokes about the shop, but never made himself useful in any way. 'You might also lend me a hand,' she said finally, as she realized that neither subtle hints nor body language can induce a man to remedy his social infirmity when it comes to being helpful.

On this occasion, even explicitly articulating one's wishes did no good. Sven seemed not to have heard. Maybe this was the case, maybe something else had absorbed every grain of his attention. Perhaps it was the missive he'd unfolded, written on paper from the elegant Zurich hotel Baur au Lac. A letter from the world-famous Viennese actor, Noé.

'Noé? Does he still live in Vienna?'

'Is he still alive in fact?'

It wasn't easy to find out whether Noé still lived in Vienna, but it wasn't important either. Thanks to Sven's smartphone, however, they were able to establish after a few minutes that he was still alive. And evidently life was rosy for Noé. He had a new wife as well as numerous, doubtlessly well-paid jobs in television. He also seemed to be a permanent guest at prize ceremonies, and the more they honoured his life's work the more tortured his expression in the photographs became.

My Dearest Charlotte,
How wonderful that package was which you sent to my little hideaway. I shall never, ever forget you for having included, besides the Thoreau and Gracidán that I requested — and which I need for a part I'm playing at the Burgtheater in Vienna — the volume of Henry James stories and Mark Twain's The Innocents Abroad. *Both writers, each in his own way, are godlike observers and windbags. 'As a general thing, we have been shown through palaces by some plush-legged filigreed flunkey or other, who charged a franc for it.' — Twain. I cried with laughter, dearest Charlotte! His experience was like that you get in a posh hotel where every few paces there's a boy who bows while holding out his hand. Polished buttons everywhere but no sense of discretion!*

Appended to this letter you will find another short list of requests which I'd be terribly grateful if you would send me. These are books I've been meaning to read for ages or ones I've lost somewhere over the course of my wandering artist's life. Please be so kind as to send them again to my mountain retreat. There's no particular hurry; I'm on tour in France for the next three weeks. But if your package were to be there on my return, it would be a source of great comfort and relaxation after the strains that such travelling and nightly performances place on a sensitive artist's heart and my permanently somewhat frail physique. Please put the books on my account and I shall pay my debts when I next visit your city.

With my warmest regards and deep respect,
Yours,
Noé

P.S. Please try to find the most beautiful editions available. A book is so much more than the sum of its words!

What couldn't be found was a list of the books. There was nothing else with the letter. But another thought had crept into Valerie's

76

mind as Sven read out the letter: she'd seen the name of the famous actor on another list — several times in fact! On the list of unpaid bills . . .

★ ★ ★

At this point, dear reader, we can't help forcing our narrator to revise his preconceived ideas. Even the most witless business economist can, in certain circumstances, be placed in a position to steer his or her imagination in some other direction than towards currencies. This doesn't mean that such circumstances will always obtain. In Sven's case, we're looking at someone whose imagination was clearly fired by monetary affairs, which is why — surrounded by countless fascinating stories — he quickly became bored in the small bookshop. 'I can't understand,' he said sulkily one evening, 'why you're wasting your time in here. It's all hopeless.'

'Sven . . . it's what my aunt wanted. We don't even know where she is. How she is . . .'

'Which means she abandoned all of this long ago, and it's high time you followed her example.' He blew some non-existent dust from a copy of *Man of Straw* and then stared morosely out into the street, where a crane was being delivered.

'What? Vanish into thin air? Great plan.'

'Don't be silly,' he carped. He wasn't in the mood for jokes. 'I mean you should abandon this.'

'Maybe she'll come back. Hopefully . . . '

'Then she can do the job herself. This slump in turnover — was it your fault or hers?'

'Instead of being so mean about Aunt Charlotte, why don't you help me?' Valerie replied, suppressing the lump that was trying to rise in her throat.

'You want help? OK then!' He turned around, went up the two steps to the office, grabbed a pen and paper and scribbled down some bullet points. Then, perched with one buttock on the edge of the desk, he pontificated, 'The first thing you ought to do is a target group analysis. Who shops in this joint?'

'OK . . . well, at the moment I'd say it's almost exclusively people who just pop in off the street. Far too few at any rate.'

'Look, if you know who you're sitting here for and which sort of people you're expecting,' Sven continued impassively, 'you're on the way to sharpening your profile. Otherwise you're missing out on at least half your ideal customers. Don't waste any time on the min-nows. If you've got three sorts of customers, concentrate on the two lucrative groups and let the third go.'

'Three sorts of customers would be great, Sven. The way things look at the moment I don't even have . . . '

'Process optimization and profit maximiza-tion,' the young man blurted out with a faint tremolo — his forehead was quivering. 'These are measures you need to undertake. A business doesn't work because you've tried to understand how others have got it wrong; it runs smoothly because you find out how you can make it work yourself.'

Although at that moment Valerie hated Sven for his perspective on things and found his pathological diagnosis ridiculous, his insight was perhaps not altogether wide of the mark. And yet, everything he'd said before that sounded so inane, and she marvelled she had ever taken all the nonsense from her course so seriously. 'Or . . . ' she said, getting up. 'Or the secret of a bookshop is something quite different.' She shoved Sven off the desk and herded him to the back door.

'Right,' Sven said laconically. 'I can see that.'

'Listen, I know myself that the shop wasn't working. But believe me, if it were as simple as you say and that all you had to do to get the cash rolling in was a target group analysis, process optimization and tralala, then any moron with a bookshop would soon be minted.'

'Thanks for calling me a moron,' Sven grumbled, half-heartedly resisting being shoved out of the door. 'Hey, what are you doing?'

'Go home, Sven. I could be here a while yet. I need more time to work my alchemy. You'll get out via the backyard.'

'Alchemy?' Sven spluttered, aghast. 'Are you mixing with poets now or . . . ?'

Valerie was very pleased when the door closed and shut out the noises coming from outside. Thrusting his hands into his coat pockets, Sven trudged off. And Valerie could have sworn that behind her an armada of books were chuckling softly.

But she wasn't happy. Somehow her relationship with Sven was not going in the right direction. Ringelnatz & Co. was to blame, quite clearly. Last year, in February, they'd considered renting a flat together instead of living separately in overpriced apartments. But no more had been said on the matter since Charlotte vanished. And while she watched Sven turn the corner and disappear from view, the image of that mysterious young man came into her head again. How differently he had left the shop. In fact, as Valerie had to admit to herself, he'd never really left it — all too often she thought she could feel his presence, all too often she could hear his voice: 'I could spend my life here.'

The lump had returned to her throat and the only way she could be rid of it was to wash it back down with a flood of tears. Valerie looked reproachfully at the books, which maintained an embarrassed silence. Finally she blew her nose, packed one of the folders with letters into the large bag she always carried around with her these days, so she could take a few books to and from home, and left the shop too. As she walked out she glimpsed Grisaille's nose poking out from behind a ledge on the wall.

'Oh, it's you,' she said, stopping. 'I didn't give you anything today . . . I'm very sorry.' The rat gave her a curious look. 'Wait.' Valerie quickly opened the shop, took a saucer from the cupboard, poured a little milk and placed it on the window sill before locking up again and standing a short distance from the window. Grisaille was not at all afraid of her; the young woman had long been a familiar face and the two of them occasionally talked to each other. Valerie noticed that the creature had become a little rounder. Was that the milk? But surely the rat's belly was growing a bit too quickly for that.

'You're pregnant!' Valerie exclaimed quietly, observing her little friend with fascination. 'Of course, it all happens rather quickly with you lot. That's why you've got so round.'

This sparked a thought in her. She picked a little red book from her bag, a collection of Robert Louis Stevenson's poems. 'Do you know this one?' she asked Grisaille. 'It's called *From a Railway Carriage*. Listen!

Faster than fairies, faster than witches,
Bridges and houses, hedges and ditches;
And charging along like troops in a battle,
All through the meadows the horses and
    cattle:
All of the sights of the hill and the plain
Fly as thick as driving rain;
And ever again, in the wink of an eye,
Painted stations whistle by.

Here is a child who clambers and scrambles,
All by himself and gathering brambles;
Here is a tramp who stands and gazes;
And there is the green for stringing the
    daisies!
Here is a cart run away in the road
Lumping along with man and load;
And here is a mill and there is a river:
Each a glimpse and gone for ever!

For some reason Valerie had to cry again the moment she stopped, perhaps because she feared she would soon lose Grisaille when the rat had to care for her babies.

She put the book down. 'I can only hope that your man has a different mentality than mine. See you tomorrow.' Ill at ease, she left the yard to go home. As lovely as the bookshop was and as attached as she had become to all those books, at times it was comforting to free herself from the burden of responsibility and nestle into the sofa at home or share a glass of wine with friends.

9

Recently she'd only been home to shower and sleep. To read in peace and have the odd coffee. But the computer in her work corner had barely been touched and her fridge had suffered from chronic emptiness — Valerie just didn't get around to shopping any more. Running a shop meant being there during business hours. But whenever she came back to her small flat — actually, a tiny flat — she was astonished at how mundane these four walls were. No samovar. No eighteen varieties of tea. No little rodent you could chat to. No faux antique reading chair. And hardly any books, or at least none apart from textbooks and a few comics that Sven had dumped at some point.

It had only taken a few days for Valerie to feel as if she were coming home whenever she entered the bookshop. Now, in this apartment, she sometimes felt like a stranger, as if it were part of someone else's life altogether, whereas Ringelnatz & Co. was part of *hers*.

Some of the letters she'd brought back were very touching. A teacher thanked Aunt Charlotte: with the book (sadly the letter didn't specify which) that the elderly lady had recommended as a class read, she'd *finally reconnected with my pupils, even though I'd never have been able to get the management to approve this novel. But maybe that was one of the reasons why — I made a pact with the class; for the time it took us to read the book we were a secret community. You know, many years ago this is exactly how I'd imagined what being a teacher would be like, before reality got in the way. But now, thanks to you, I know that there are other realities!*

Valerie couldn't argue with that. Sven, for example, had a completely different reality from hers. And this flat had a completely different reality from Aunt Charlotte's bookshop.

Another letter was written in beautifully looped handwriting and in pale-blue ink:

Dear Bookseller,
If you receive this letter I hope to be standing on the roof of the world. It is to be the final stop on a long journey you have unknowingly sent me on. Although many a night I've wondered whether you had any idea what you were doing by entrusting this book to me — this magical, unbelievable, disorienting story, which quite unexpectedly

became my story. I've been following it for almost a year now, chapter by chapter, stage by stage, and I'm discovering how my life could have been too. No! How it became. Thanks to you, my dear! You changed everything for me, for you gave me this book, which has made my dreams come true and continues to do so. Sometimes I read ahead, but I don't dare find out the ending. Sometimes I flick back and remember it all again. But now there's not much left and I know that soon I'll be returning to everyday life, where we'll hopefully meet again. But everyday life as I knew it from before will no longer exist. No, I know that I'll celebrate every day of my life until the end of my days. If I were to have another ten years on this planet of ours, I'd wish to receive ten books like this and read each one differently. But I shall enjoy the uncertainty and launch myself with relish into every adventure.

Thank you, thank you, thank you!
With warmest regards,
Yours,

Gertje Zurhoven

Valerie would have loved to know the unsurpassable book that her aunt had commended to Frau Zurhoven. But there was nothing about it in the letter. The customer seemed to have spent an entire year reading the novel. It was hard to imagine that a single book could take so long, unless it was the Bible. Interestingly, this was not the only letter that mentioned a year in relation to a book. Another missive, penned by a young hand, Valerie found oddly moving.

Dear Charlotte (thanks for allowing me to call you this),
When I entered the clinic a year ago I thought my life was over. I couldn't imagine being in a wheelchair for ever. Tomorrow, on my fourteenth birthday, I'm going to be discharged. I'm still in a wheelchair and maybe I'll always have to be. But now I know that my life isn't over. I'm so grateful you gave my mum this book for me. I've read it again and again, throughout the entire year that I've had to stay in the clinic. To begin with your book was the only thing that kept me alive. My mum read it out to me. At the start I found it very difficult to concentrate. But then, at some point, I was right in the

heart of the story, as if it was my own story. I've dreamed every dream in the book and from the window I've seen every person that's been written about. Soon I started reading myself and discovered so many good things in the book that I've come to love life. I love it far more than before my accident. I love it so much that I'm almost grateful it all happened to me. It might sound crazy, but that's how I feel. As I write this I can see a few specks of dust dancing in the sunlight. There ought not to be any dust in the room at all. But this ballet's so wonderful that I'm glad a little 'dirt' has been left. When I was still 'healthy' I saw almost nothing at all, noticed nothing and didn't think about anything. I didn't even have dreams, not proper ones. Now I've got all of this. And I feel that only now do I understand how wonderful it is to be alive. I've got you to thank for this. You ought to know how much you've given me. Thanks.
Yours,

Nina F.

Valerie made herself a cup of coffee in her old espresso pot. It rattled a bit and hissed, then an aroma unfolded that immediately reminded her of her mother, who always made coffee like this in the old days, when Valerie still lived in an ideal world, in childhood, at home, at a time when Papa wasn't the cynic he'd become, but every year would make himself look ridiculous as Father Christmas, every year would build snowmen with Valerie and make children's punch at New Year, when on her birthday he'd climb to the top of the cathedral with her and each summer sit cursing in traffic so they could spend a carefree holiday together in the south. When every year the cherry tree in the garden would blossom and every year a photo was taken of Valerie with the girl next door. When every year at Easter the house smelled of raisin bread and Mama cooked up fruit in autumn. All the years had passed like this and nobody had noticed how wonderful they'd been. And Valerie had noticed least of all. She wished she knew what had become of the girl who'd written this letter. But there was no address on it, not even a complete name.

She sat back down with her coffee on the sofa bed, which she hadn't made back into a sofa for weeks, only changing the sheets occasionally, and placed the folder with the letters on her lap again. As she went through the papers she noticed to her astonishment that the famous actor, whose letter Sven had read out in the shop, hadn't just written one letter to her aunt.

My Dear Charlotte,
I arrived back home in my beloved
mountains the day before Christmas
Eve. How thrilled I was to find your
package of books there, far more trea-
sured than all the Christmas presents
I'd already been sent. But what on
earth are you trying to say to me with
this sentimental Letter from an
Unknown Woman *by Stefan Zweig*
(whom I otherwise hold in high
esteem)!? Do you not know that I'm
one of the most melancholy individuals
under the sun? I found more appealing
the laconic humour of the Alan Bennett
book you included. But nothing comes
close to his Uncommon Reader, *not*
even this magnificent, sad yet funny
Clothes *farce*

The famous actor proceeded to discuss his ill-nesses and unhappy (that's to say: unsuccessful) love affairs (that's to say: conquests). Although the letter was brimming with compliments and flattery, it was utterly narcissistic too. If he expressed his thanks, it was a pretext to show off his knowledge; if he asked for forgiveness, he was fishing for sympathy; if he sounded contrite, it was an exercise in vanity. Valerie was just about to consign the vulgar missive to the waste-paper basket when she caught sight of the unduly long postscript:

How fondly I think back to those sweet evenings in the séparée you created in your delightful little shop, the wine and the tenderness between us. Oh, if only we were twenty years younger, if only it were thirty years ago! But after all these long years I no longer dare pay court to you and disclose my infatuation. No, in your mind's eye you should see me as you once gazed at me with your black diamonds. And with every bar of Shostakovich I listen out for your heartbeat as I once did behind your shamelessly red curtain in those fair hours of our first life. Do you still have the gramophone? Oh, I'm sure it's gone now, like so much else. Gone and lost for all time. I send you my love with tears in my eyes. Yours,

Noé

What a bombshell! Aunt Charlotte as the
decadent lover of a great actor and notorious
philanderer? Aunt Charlotte? 'I don't believe
it!' Valerie stammered more than once as she
paced up and down the flat, the letter in her
hand. 'Aunt Charlotte — Noé's sweetheart?
The Noé?' All of a sudden she saw the shop
through quite different eyes. The curtain, yes,
she'd drawn it too, when Sven . . . The
armchair in which they'd . . . Did her aunt
. . . Surely that wasn't possible. Was it? After
all, elderly ladies haven't always been elderly
ladies. And if thirty years ago, several years
before Valerie was born . . . Well, Aunt
Charlotte would have been around fifty at the
time, so in all probability still a woman with
undeniable charms.

'Auntie, Auntie,' Valerie muttered, sinking
onto her sofa bed. 'Who would have thought
it?'

10

Management consultancies like their employees to spend some time abroad. It improves their skill with modern languages, sharpens their sensibility for the globalized market and imbues future executives with a certain cosmopolitanism. Most of all, of course, it prevents young employees from putting down firm roots. For anyone who gets attached early, let alone brings offspring into the world, will become unwieldy for business use and start articulating ever greater demands vis-à-vis employment rights, which are generally an obstacle to commercial demands.

Now, there are some strong personalities who avoid being completely swallowed up by their firm, and who follow their heart rather than their career. And there are those who we'll later applaud as heroes of industry, extolling their courage, application, entrepreneurial genius and consistent self-sacrifice.

Regrettably, it is impossible to deny that Sven fell into the latter category. If till now no meeting had been too late, no business dinner too unnecessary and no work trip too long, the offer to go to Doha 'for a few months and, if you do well, maybe even for longer' was utterly irresistible. Doha, the capital of Qatar on the Persian Gulf. It didn't only sound exotic and unrelated to virtually anything he'd heard of before, most of all it sounded like a hefty salary rise and an extension to his contract by a year at least.

And so one July evening — it was beautifully warm, she'd put a chair outside the shop, a bottle of wine beside it (and a glass, of course) and had just opened a wonderful little book — Valerie received a text on her mobile: 'Doha's happening! Yeah!'

'Great!' she texted back. 'I'm delighted for you.' Then she deleted the second sentence. She turned 'Great!' into 'Great', and 'Great' into 'Wow!', then 'Wow' and finally . . .

She poured herself another glass of wine, swirled it around and held it up to her nose. As the bouquet of blackberries, lavender, fir, oak and vanilla roamed her senses, she watched a family walking down the street some distance away. The wife was wearing a headscarf, the man had a beard, the boy an enormous stick of candy floss, so large that his entire head disappeared behind it. She looked up at the lit window opposite, through which she could see the silhouette of a woman moving back and forth. Maybe she was mixing something in a bowl, maybe she was playing guitar or piano, maybe she was sitting on her boyfriend. Whatever she was doing, it looked as if she was doing it with commitment. The family soon vanished. The glass soon emptied. The light in the window switched off. Valerie turned off her mobile. 'Have a good flight,' she muttered, opening her book in the weak light of dusk, which coalesced with the weak light of the streetlamp. And as a soft summer wind took all thoughts of Sven away, so these words took her to another place at another time:

Snow-Balls have flown their Arcs, starr'd the Sides of Outbuildings, as of Cousins, carried Hats away into the brisk Wind off Delaware — the Sleds are brought in and their Runners carefully dried and greased, shoes deposited in the back Hall, a stocking'd-foot Descent made upon the great Kitchen . . .

She has more than a thousand pages before her. Her first really thick book. It's not one of those must-reads her aunt had catalogued without any notes. No, on this one she commented simply, 'The most beautiful first line in all literature. The entire book one long poem.'

It may well turn out to be a book that's

impossible to explain, one like James Joyce's *Ulysses* that is as compelling as it is unreadable, so mysterious and puzzling that after reading it what lingers is the uncertain feeling of having gained a glimpse of an unheard-of world rather than the certainty of having understood its life and workings.

Aunt Charlotte had also made a note on Joyce's masterpiece: 'Liebig's Extract of Meat. You can't eat it. But it'll make many soups (Tucholsky).'

There were a few similarly gargantuan tomes, which Valerie had put in a separate pile to turn to in moments of hubris. Thomas Mann's *The Magic Mountain* was there, as were Gabriel García Márquez's *One Hundred Years of Solitude*, Robert Musil's *The Man without Qualities*, Jonathan Franzen's *The Corrections*, David Foster Wallace's *Infinite Jest* and Susanna Clarke's *Jonathan Strange and Mr Norell* (Aunt Charlotte's comment: 'As if from another time. A great storyteller!') Each one a heavyweight and out of the ordinary. Literary bulk. Valerie was terrified of these works. But as the old truism goes, fear always shows the way. And so, whenever she'd had enough of the monotony of management, she followed the path of fear and leaped into the adventures of these mighty literary tomes.

And that was what she did that evening, when she'd had enough of managing her relationship with Sven, in which there were no more surprises (had there ever been any?), in which passion had long given way to sex (had there ever been any passion?), in which almost every conversation revolved around benchmarks, liquidity management or entre-preneurship (had these been conversations?). She could have granted herself a short period of mourning, to allow the grass to grow over their separation. Instead she seized Thomas Pynchon's *Mason & Dixon* and let stories as finely knit and flighty as just-hatched butterflies swarm over the matter. And while she plunged deep into the obscure tale of two land surveyors, above her, on the surface, a young man drifted away. But we can dispense with him for the rest of our story.

★　★　★

Summer bestowed bright, sunny days and mild evenings on the city. The neighbourhood came pleasantly alive. People from all corners of the world sat in small and sometimes larger groups outside the shops, chatting away, often late into the night. All of a sudden Valerie was no longer an outsider with her table and tea in front of the house. Occasionally someone might come past and offer her an exotic sweet (which was always far too sweet) or invite her to sit with the others. For example the owners of the Gülestan Market, which exuded its oriental aromas a few doors down, in the shade of a huge awning. Nice people, hard to understand with their funny accents, the men reserved in a friendly way; the women far more open. But all of them displayed a warmth that Valerie had never come across before, not even in her own family. And so they got along well, joking, laughing, drinking tea (on the second visit Valerie brought a mixture from Aunt Charlotte's collection) and gratefully lauding the wonderful summer, which reminded each of them of a different place — for one it would be their home in Izmir, another his childhood by the sea. For Valerie, however, it reminded her of *Emil of Lönneberga*, a story that her mother read to her as a young girl, when summer was always sunny and carefree.

★ ★ ★

And then a handwritten letter arrived, which — in a script as spirited as it was meticulous — was not addressed to Aunt Charlotte, but to *The enchanting young lady c/o Ringelnatz & Co.*, and which plunged

Valerie into emotional turmoil. It was a short letter and enclosed was a small book:

Dear Stranger,
I came across this delightful epistolary
novel in a small bookshop in Prague. I
had to think of you (as I do almost
every time I step into a bookshop) and
hope I can remotely give you a little
pleasure by sending it to you. Perhaps
you don't remember me. No, you cer-
tainly won't remember me. But in your
shop I found a book I'd been unsuc-
cessfully trying to track down for ages,
as only a few copies of it exist: A Very
Special Year. Without knowing it, you
have changed my life and I will always
carry you around with me — you can
guess where. If I were Cyrano, I'd dare
do it . . .
With heartfelt greetings —

The signature was illegible as if he'd written it in a different alphabet.

Valerie sat in silence, staring at the writing, which oozed sophistication and intelligence. It was a while before she opened the short book: *84 Charing Cross Road* by Helene Hanff. But she was unable to read. She couldn't get out of her head the picture of the

99

young man who'd appeared in her shop as suddenly as he'd disappeared into the night. She picked up the envelope and turned it over. But there was no return address.

A soft sound from the back window wrenched her from her thoughts. A scraping, a scratching, barely audible. 'Oh, Grisaille,' Valerie sighed, opening the window and gazing into the tiny, shining eyes of her old friend. She poured some milk into a saucer and placed it on the sill. The rat didn't have her old figure back yet, but she'd clearly had her children. 'Congratulations,' Valerie said. 'I bet you're happy.'

⋆　⋆　⋆

Of course the occasional customer came into the shop, and even bought books. Once an elderly lady in a flowery Laura Ashley dress browsed the shelves and took a large pile of children's books for her grandchildren (she was mindful to let Valerie advise her as thoroughly as possible, before making her own, arbitrary selection, which bore no relation to Valerie's recommendations). She requested the books be sent to her home, which gave Valerie the opportunity to make the acquaintance of a rather rundown but grand villa near the Stadtpark, along with a harmless yet absolutely terrifying dog that protected the property and its distinguished owner.

To begin with, Valerie had harboured the suspicion that this customer might be another of those ladies who liked shopping but disliked paying. After all, her scrutiny of the cashbooks and list of unsettled bills showed that the shop was owed a whopping 28,000 euros, an incomprehensibly large sum, not even taking into account the interest and compound interest. For far too long Valerie had done nothing to address this. But on her way back from visiting the old lady she took a decision. Perhaps she was emboldened by the inevitability of transience, perhaps it was simply desperation. For too little money was going through the till and, even if costs were being kept down, a certain level of income was needed just to survive. Valerie's bank account had been in the red for two weeks. She was earning next to nothing and the gridlock in her financial affairs would soon spell serious trouble. Sure, she could have asked her father. But she didn't want to. Of all the solutions that occurred to her, this was the one that was out of the question. For her father would regard her as a poor economist, as he had Aunt Charlotte. The difference was that her aunt dismissed the criticism with a shrug of her shoulders and a gentle smile, whereas it would hurt Valerie. No, there were other solutions.

Back in the shop she sat at the desk and took out the folder with the letters of thanks, as well as the one containing the outstanding bills. She didn't have to spend long looking, nor spend long thinking about it. On a sheet of the wonderfully old-fashioned Ringelnatz & Co. writing paper, and under the watchful eye of a young mother of six lovely little rats, she began her letter:

Dear Herr Noé . . .

11

Summer is a difficult time for the book trade. Although people do read on holiday, they buy few books. Their summer reading is sorted out in spring-time, and now they get down to it. From time to time the Gülestan greengrocer's daughter came by, a likeable teenager with fabulous locks of black hair that she only just kept under control beneath a rather fashionable headscarf. But she was more interested in chatting to Valerie than in books. In any case, very few of the things she wanted to read were available in Aunt Charlotte's shop. Although Valerie noted down the girl's orders — she answered to the beautiful name Siba — she wasn't sure about stocking those sorts of books permanently. Not because they were too lowbrow (who, seriously, was in a position to make a judgement here?) but because she sensed it might upset the delicate structure by which the shop was arranged.

The more time she spent here, the more strongly she became aware of the bookshop's highly individual character. Had it belonged to her, she wouldn't have hesitated to change this character. But she still clung to the hope that Aunt Charlotte would turn up again someday. So she took down Siba's orders and passed them onto the incredibly reliable and prompt warehouse of Charlotte's distributor. She drank a cup of the Turkish tea that the girl had brought along so she could chat to Valerie about whether Istanbul was a modern city, whether she ought to read Turkish books in Turkish or German (although she quite clearly had no interest in Turkish books, unlike Valerie who'd suddenly become engrossed in Orhan Pamuk's *My Name is Red*) and what school the boy might go to who'd recently started delivering for Pronto Pizza at weekends (and who she was probably keen on).

So the months passed and the year moved on imperceptibly, and Valerie's bookkeeping skills developed without her having paid much thought to the matter. She'd long abandoned the idea of liquidating the business; now the idea seemed absolutely absurd to her. After all, Aunt Charlotte had not said 'Close my shop down!'; she had merely requested that Valerie look after it. And that's what she was doing. Through the whole of spring and summer.

★ ★ ★

She first noticed him one Monday in September. As if he'd appeared out of thin air, there he was standing in front of the shop window, slightly to one side. She could barely see him behind the gathered curtain. His face was narrow, perhaps a little pale too. But his eyes twinkled with curiosity, examining the display in great detail, much more intensely than anyone else who'd stopped to look during the time that Valerie had been in charge. Peering more closely she could see his lips moving very faintly.

After that he turned up every day. Every school day, to be precise. Valerie guessed he must be in the fourth or fifth class; it was hard to say. Sometimes he'd pause briefly as he passed the door, then move on to study the window just as thoroughly from the other side, which amazed Valerie as the display hardly ever changed, nor were there any children's books there. 'Why not, actually?' she thought, having watched the boy on another occasion, and so she decided to include books for younger readers in the display too, as well as rotating the items on show more frequently. If she were now running the shop there was no reason to feature just the books her aunt had selected, for whatever good or trivial reason.

And so one day the boy allowed his keen

and inquisitive gaze to wander along a new row of books in the window, evidently excited by the collection of unfamiliar reading matter suddenly before him. Finally his eyes stopped at an attractive little volume on the very end of the display, where Valerie had placed a copy of Kate DiCamillo's *The Tale of Despereaux*.

The boy would come past every day at lunchtime, obviously on his way home, so it was not hard to catch him. Behind the cover of the large curtain Valerie had an excellent vantage point from which to observe him. She couldn't help but smile and thought back to her own childhood and adolescence. Yes, there had been days when she'd absolutely devoured books, one after the other, and when she'd come to the end of her supplies she simply reread what was there and then again.

The following day something extraordinary happened. The boy came *in* to the shop. Not tentatively; he entered without a hint of timidity, put his satchel down by the door and looked around in the gloomy light. Valerie had been expecting the boy and watched him, partially hidden behind a tall library ladder in the antiquarian section.

Closing his eyes, the boy breathed in deeply the air inside the shop. Then he nodded approvingly and turned to the nearest shelf. 'Can I help you?' Valerie asked, stepping out from behind her ladder.

'No thanks, that's not necessary,' the boy replied slightly precociously. 'I'm just having a look around.'

'Fine. If you need me I'll be in the office.' She pointed to the stairs then headed off in that direction to do a bit of bookkeeping.

Out of the corner of her eye she watched the boy inspect the titles on the book spines. 'Children's books are at the front on the left, beside the door,' she called out.

'OK,' was all he said, ignoring her as he took out an E.T.A. Hoffmann work and leafed through it, followed by some Hemingway short stories and then Camus's *The Outsider* . . . He inspected each volume with the greatest of care, opening it, stroking the paper with his fingertips, turning it over, taking off the dust jacket and caressing the ribbon marker if the book had one . . . He delved into Kant for a long while, came across Eichendorff (who he took a close look at) beside the armchair and then was engrossed for ages in Jonathan Sáfran Foer's *Tree of Codes*, a book so weird and complicated that it had completely bewildered Valerie when she'd browsed through it. After spending a long time with this obscure marvel of modern American literature, he shut it and put it down beside his satchel.

Valerie cleared her throat. 'Would you mind putting it back on the shelf, please?'

But the boy just casually raised his hand and, over his shoulder, aimed an 'I'm taking it' in Valerie's direction. The Foer was joined by a collection of Daniil Kharms' writing, Maupassant's *Bel Ami* and the *Gilgamesh* epic.

It was almost evening by the time the boy stood next to her with his bundle of books and said drily, 'I'd like these.'

Valerie tried to fathom from his expression whether he was being serious. If he was joking, this young customer had the poker face of the century.

'Have you got that much money?'

'Seventy-four euros, thirty-nine cents? Sure.'

'Hmm.' Valerie took the books from him and put them on the desk. She entered the prices into the ancient till and tapped with the back of her hand the enter key, which for some inexplicable reason had 'CASH' written on it vertically. When she'd rung up all the prices she pressed 'CASH' again and stared at the display, a small, unglazed window behind which black cogs with engraved white numbers rotated. It told her: 'Seventy-four euros, thirty-nine cents.'

The boy felt in his trouser pocket and pulled out a twenty-euro note. 'That's what I can pay,' he told her, handing over the banknote.

'I see. I'm afraid I can't put it on account.'

'On account?'

'Lend you the money.'

'You don't have to lend me any money,' the boy said, unfazed. 'Basically you're just lending me the books. Until I've paid them off in full. Then they'll belong to me.'

'Erm . . . sure,' Valerie replied, ambushed by the logic of his reasoning.

And before she could lay down any further clear rules on the subject of payment by instalment, the boy nodded and said, 'So we're agreed. I pass by here every day anyway. If I've got any money I'll just give you some.'

Suddenly it dawned on Valerie what had happened. Only now did she realize. 'You're making fun of me!' She laughed, still slightly uncertain, but she laughed. 'This is a joke, right? You'd never ever be interested in these books. How old are you, anyway?'

'Ten. And you?'

'Twenty- . . . OK — erm — young man, leading me up the garden path like that is all very cute, but I'd like to shut the shop now and go home.'

'Oh blimey!' the boy replied. 'Home. I'd completely forgotten! Mum's going to be worried. Then she'll have a go at me because she loves me so much.' He picked up the books to put them in his bag.

'Wait a moment,' Valerie called out. 'That's enough now, OK? Please leave the books where they are; I'll put them back myself. Here's your twenty euros back . . . ' She held out the banknote, but he merely looked at it, vaguely disconcerted.

'But I bought the books.'

'Yes, but you weren't being serious . . . '

'I *was*.' And with that the books vanished into his schoolbag, which he threw over his shoulder.

'Now look here . . . ' With a determined stride she overtook him and blocked his way to the door. 'What do you want with Kharms? And Maupassant? You're ten years old! Kids your age read children's books, *not* old French novelists. Nor contemporary experimental American literature.'

'Experimental?' She couldn't fail to notice the gleam in his eyes.

What's going through his head now? Valerie wondered, but somehow she was struck by an unbelievable sympathy for the boy who'd come into her shop with such confidence, trawled through the collection of books, handed over all his money and was now standing here in front of her like a

110

gentlemanly philosopher thrust back into childhood. His eyes were so full of curiosity and disarming attentiveness that Valerie suddenly felt ashamed. She cleared her throat, pointed to his satchel and asked, 'Why these books? Why not *Desperaux*? Or *Charlie and the Chocolate Factory*?'

'These were the most beautiful.'

'The most beautiful?'

'Yes.' He unfastened his satchel, took out the English-language book by Foer and opened it up. 'Look, the pages have holes you can read the individual words through. If you turn over the page you discover other words. Everything keeps changing, depending on how you look at it. That's cool! I've never seen a book like that before. And the other ones are beautiful too. This one here,' he said, pulling out the *Gilgamesh* a fraction, 'has got two cords.'

'Ribbon markers.'

'Yes. A red one and a silver one. I like that. It's completely different from how it usually is.'

'Usually?'

'Usually things that aren't particularly special are packaged really nicely to make them look good. With books it's the other way round. The packaging can never be as amazing as the stories. Well, sometimes the packaging *can* be beautiful too, and then you don't just enjoy reading the book but also holding it in your hand and gazing at it. But I've got to go!' And with that he was out the door and vanishing into the twilight.

Valerie just stood there, watching him run past the other shops where all they did was put ordinary things in extraordinary packages. She'd never looked at it like that. In a bookshop the beauty of the form could never compete with the diversity and uniqueness of what was packaged therein. What was extraordinary about a book was what was inside it.

★   ★   ★

The boy, who was called Timmi ('with two 'I's like in Indonesia'), continued to pop in every day. He browsed, read, sat in the armchair and did actually bury himself in the DiCamillo until he'd finished the book. Sometimes he had a bit of money on him, which he'd use to pay off another part of his debt. He was, in fact, a quite ordinary boy, as well as being a quite extraordinary one. Time and again he'd baffle Valerie with his insights into literature, which were characterized by the fact that he saw things from completely different perspectives, perspectives which would never have occurred to Valerie.

'How many books do you actually have here?' he once asked.

'Around eight thousand.'

'Eight thousand different books . . . ' Timmi repeated in acknowledgement.

'Hold on a sec. I've got more than one copy of many books.'

Timmi nodded. 'Either way it's still just a tiny proportion of all possible books.'

'All possible books?'

'Altogether there can be 26 to the power of 26 books.'

'Twenty-six to the power of 26. Hmm. Because there are 26 letters, you mean?'

'That's right. Of course there could be many, many more books if you include all the other languages with different alphabets. But if you combine every letter with every other letter . . . '

'Then you get 26 to the power of 26 possibilities of writing a book. What about letters with umlauts — Ä, Ö and Ü?'

'You're right, and the double S: ß. That makes it 30 to the power of thirty.'

'Sounds about right,' Valerie said, shaking her head with a smile. She'd never really thought of it like that before.

Timmi sighed. 'Sounds wrong to me somehow. I expect you also have to multiply it with the number of pages and lines . . . '

'Number of characters!' Valerie suggested.

'Yes. Or you have to times it by the number of characters: 26 x x is the number of characters in the entire book. But I suppose you have to include spaces and punctuation marks in the calculation as well. Somehow.'

'In any case it sounds rather complicated,' Valerie said.

'Oh, maths is easy. Because everything always follows the rules. That's why I like books. There are always surprises!'

Valerie nodded. 'And we've got thousands of them here,' she said, winking at him. 'You won't find a range like this in any other kind of shop.'

'Well,' Timmi said, 'actually you only sell thirty different types of goods.'

Valerie laughed. 'True. We've got everything here, but only from A to Z.'

As dubious as all their mathematical deliberations had been, this conclusion was indisputably correct.

12

One fine autumn day, Valerie put her table and chair outside again and finally fetched a book by the man after whom her shop was named. That morning she'd been visited by two publishing reps and listened while they presented their forthcoming schedules. Time and again she was overwhelmed by the abundance of new books; it was a vast deluge through which she needed these pilots of the literature industry to steer her, but even so she never stopped fearing she would drown in the torrent. She could do with a little cheerful relaxation. Contrary to her expectations, however, Ringelnatz's poems and ideas were not only silly and humorous, they often had melancholy at their heart and an affectionate, but essentially pessimistic sophistry. Life was no cakewalk. Not for him, nor for anybody else on this earth.

And so Valerie, who'd wanted to blink in the sun and be cheered up by a few light verses, soon found herself in the gloominess of her own mood, watching the construction workers across the street and ruminating on the futility and transience of all human activity.

Until Timmi turned the corner, discovered the book on the table, looked up at the sign above the shop, rocked his head comically from side to side like an Indian street trader and declared, 'I think it's interesting that your shop's called 'Ringelnatz and so'.'

'Ringelnatz & Co.,' she corrected him.

'It's a complicated name.'

'Well, not really. It's the name of a writer,' Valerie explained, as she watched Timmi sit on the doorstep beside her. 'And Co. means that it's not just Ringelnatz's books that are sold here, but those by other writers too.'

'Then it was this writer who had the complicated name. Has it got anything to do with ringlets?'

'I don't know. But anyway, it's a pseudonym. Would you like a cup of tea?'

'Yes, but lots of milk, please.'

'Of course!' She went inside, poured tea from the samovar pot — not too much, because Timmi was only ten — then filled it half-way up the cup with water, and then topped up with milk from the small fridge in the office. 'You know what a pseudonym is, don't you?'

Timmi nodded. 'I've heard of it before. It's not difficult to imagine what it is either. Even though it's not Latin. More like Greek I think.'

'Do you do Latin at school?'

'Uh-huh. It's my favourite subject. I can tell *you* that.'

Valerie had to smile to herself. She knew exactly what he meant. If he admitted it to his classmates he'd immediately be branded a swot and would lose all credibility. On the other hand, he came across as a loner anyway. Other boys his age didn't hang around in bookshops all afternoon, admiring books for their aesthetic appeal.

'It could mean: the one born with ringlets. *Natz*, I mean. From *natus*, born.'

'Nice idea,' Valerie said, realizing how much she'd come to like this boy. Whenever he didn't pop in, she caught herself glancing at the door to see whether he might not turn up after all. Whenever she was sorting through books and discovered one that looked particularly unusual, she'd put it on the little table beside the armchair so that he'd find it on his next visit. Whenever it rained, she hoped he'd remembered to bring an umbrella. Timmi had become part of this strange state of affairs that had taken her through summer and into autumn, and now the question of how this whole business could possibly be brought to a successful conclusion was a matter of urgency.

When Valerie saw Timmi standing in the

doorway the following day (it wasn't raining, nor had there been any spectacular book discovery), she grabbed a cup and filled it with tea and milk without asking him. The boy took the cup with a smile and a nod, appearing completely at home, and looked at her inquisitively.

'I've been doing a bit of research into Ringelnatz. You know . . . ' Valerie said.

'The pseudonym.'

'Yes. Well, Ringelnatz himself claimed that the name had no significance. He chose it because he liked the sound of it.' She took a cup of tea too and sat in the armchair, while Timmi perched on the stool. 'But there are clever people who have other theories. Some argue that the name comes from a ring snake.'

'A snake?'

'A very special snake. It's equally at home on land as it is in water. I think that sounds quite plausible. At any rate, Ringelnatz did spend some time at sea.'

'Was he a sailor?'

'Yup.'

'Cool.' Timmi sniffed his tea then took a sip, as if he'd got lost in a Jane Austen novel and was now able to play the part of the Earl of Somewhere. 'What about the other theory?'

'Oh . . . well that's linked to a sailor's term: ringelnass.'

Timmi said nothing and drank his tea.

'Ringelnass is a common sailors' term for a seahorse.'

'I like that theory. I don't like the idea of a writer calling himself after a snake. But a seahorse, that suits.' He put his cup smartly onto the table, said, 'Thanks. I must be off.' and disappeared without having so much as glanced at a single book.

★ ★ ★

Timmi still owed four euros when his visits to the little bookshop ceased. He simply stopped coming. Once Valerie thought she saw him running past on the opposite side of the street, but by the time she'd got to the door, the boy was nowhere to be seen. It was several weeks before the peculiar barrenness that his absence generated was overgrown again with the regularity of her daily routine and the irregularities of life. Perhaps he'd moved, perhaps he'd discovered another passion. Perhaps his pocket money had stopped and he was ashamed of his debts (although Valerie would have been very happy to waive the sum he still owed). But although Timmi would soon become a mere footnote in the history of Ringelnatz & Co., something of him remained: an enthusiasm for seeing things in a very different way from usual.

13

Life sometimes proves to be an accumulation of events following on thick and fast from each other, sometimes appears as a wild vortex of barely manageable demands, often as chaos, but the elements of life always follow a very particular order: they take place consecutively. Every moment is followed by another and another and yet another until your time's up — and even after that it goes on and on, in a neat sequence.

The book has developed an incomparable form for turning this natural sequence of events into a natural concurrence. If you read a book from the first line to the last, it adheres to the conventional pattern of all existence. But sometimes we might open a book in the middle, fix on a sentence and then read from there, as a guest in the future, so to speak. Some books even ask to be opened at random. Then they throw out an idea such as:

He who ordained, when first the world began,
Time, that was not before creation's

hour,
Divided it, and gape the sun's high
power
To rule the one, the moon the other
span.

Valerie was struck by how Michelangelo's words had been translated and made anew for a different time by John Addington Symonds.

Valerie became increasingly accustomed to opening books wherever she fancied. She'd get curious and would investigate what was happening at the same time at a completely different point in the story. She could have warned Anna Karenina (another of those books that the elderly bookseller had made no comments on). She could have helped Nicholas Nickleby or Harry Potter. She would have fallen hopelessly in love with Mr Darcy and she would have cheered on Hal Jam from Kotzwinkle's cryptic parable, *The Bear Went over the Mountain*.

Occasionally she'd put the book she was reading down on the little table outside the shop, close her eyes for a moment, listen to life going on around her, think of her old aunt or Sven (although rarely of Sven these days), before picking up the book again and reading on from where the wind had blown it.

Sometimes this would allow her to rediscover a part she'd already read, but more importantly discover it in a new way; sometimes she found herself in a completely different scene, leaping straight into it as if it were a life that till then had been completely alien to her. Discovering a book meant freely rising above the demands of everyday life and uprooting your own existence from the here and now in order to plant it elsewhere.

★ ★ ★

It was the day on which the letter from the university arrived. She had failed to re-register at the beginning of the semester. Now she was informed very prosaically that she'd been ex-matriculated. Valerie ought to have been expecting this. But she simply hadn't thought about it. To tell the truth, thoughts of the university hadn't crossed her mind at all. A mistake. For now reality was striking back with merciless bureaucracy.

The note lay on the desk like a tax bill or like a love letter from the most stupid boy in the class. It made her feel aggressive. What had she done wrong to make them chuck her out just like that? OK, she'd missed a few tests, but she could retake them next semester or the one after that. She'd skipped a few seminars — in fact, all of them — but there was no consistent rule about obligatory attendance. If in the end she knew everything reasonably well she could get her credits and take the exam, maybe even obtain a better grade than if she'd hung around the campus the whole time slurping cappuccinos from the vending machine. In any case, what she was doing here was nothing other than applied business management — the practical application of what she could only learn in theory at university. In other words, it was far more important, it was learning by doing, it was real! 'Damn it!' she exclaimed, scrunching up the letter before propelling it with all her strength beyond the waste-paper basket. 'What am I now? Student? Business economist? Bachelorette?' She stood up, took a deep breath, suppressed the tears she could feel welling up, and sighed. Was that six semesters squandered? All her studies a waste of time? And for what? Without the opportunity to turn her bachelor's degree in to a master's, she could forget all her dreams of a great career in consultancy.

She turned around and fired an accusatory look at the books, which still stood stoically on their shelves, as if none of this had anything to do with them. They were all facing in a different direction. None seemed to give two figs about how human beings really felt. How she felt! Just a moment ago she'd still been a student. And now?

'And now?'

She reached for her coat, took the key from the desk and only a few seconds later was out the door, where a soft mist was weaving golden arcs around the lantern. 'And now? What am I now?' she whispered. The street was empty. The shop windows gave off a lonely glow. Mr Pronto Pizza. Nailzz. GoFit! Gülestan Market. Ringelnatz & Co. She could have laughed. Yes, it really was a joke. A bookshop in this location in this era, full of the best and most beautiful volumes, all the knowledge and imagination which the cultures of the world had produced over centuries and millennia. It was so laughable that she could do nothing but laugh as she stared at the old sign above the shop, whose gold leaf looked like a greeting from distant epochs. But then it struck her: this bookshop could only exist here and now. It was needed precisely here and now. Here and now she'd look after it, breathe new life into this old business. For here and now she realized what she had become: 'I'm a bookseller.'

★   ★   ★

There's a huge difference between tackling something with the intention of bringing it to a satisfactory conclusion and deciding to give it a new beginning. Till now Valerie had seen herself as the person who'd been given the thankless task of winding up Aunt Charlotte's affairs. But when, that previous evening, she'd stood outside in the twilight and surveyed the bleakness of the area, she suddenly realized that the carcass was still breathing. Weren't the corners of the mouth still twitching, as if the corpse was secretly making fun of the young woman?

Several things may have stifled Ringelnatz & Co.'s business: the changes in the area, the large bookshop one underground station away, internet shopping, e-books. All of these were developments that made it difficult for a business run in such an old-fashioned way to survive. But why, Valerie wondered, shouldn't I try to give this wonderful bookshop the kiss of life and wake it from its deep slumber?

And she began to see the shop through different eyes: the eyes of passers-by who might just glimpse Ringelnatz & Co. from the corner of their eyes, or who merely looked at the shop window on the way to work as they might glance up at the clock on the church tower, even though they knew precisely that they'd left home at 7.50, so it must now be

126

7.53, as it was every day of the year that they went into the office. But what, Valerie speculated, would happen if one day the clock on the church tower said 9.20? Or if it suddenly had three hands? What if the things they expected to see weren't there, but something surprising caught their eye and thus their attention?

The first thing that Valerie did was take everything out of the display window and close the curtain.

★ ★ ★

Valerie worked from the inside out. To start with she changed the lighting to make it brighter, yet more romantic. She did this by covering the ceiling lights, which were permanently off because they were ghastly fluorescent tubes, with a red and an orange cloth. Switched on, they now made the shop appear friendly and inviting, as if it were Christmas every day. Then she repositioned the stool, covering it with a tablecloth and adorning it with individual books that she considered good reads as well as beautiful. She arranged more seating opportunities and revamped the shop window, creating a mysterious display by cutting large keyholes in book-size pieces of black cardboard and placing them on top of the books

127

displayed so that only a section of the cover — the most attractive — was visible. Above these she hung colourful pieces of paper with letters that spelled out:

I-f y-o-u w-a-n-t t-o f-i-n-d o-u-t m-o-r-e . . .

And she repainted the sign above the entrance. Like an Irish pub, the golden letters now shone on a deep green background: Ringelnatz & Co.

And indeed over the coming days a few passers-by were caught in the web that Valerie had woven. Some of these even became customers, including a teacher (at Timmi's school?) who appeared delighted that in times like these such a young woman would dare take on a bookshop and fly the sacred banner of culture (she didn't use these exact words, of course, and Valerie omitted to reveal how she'd embarked on this adventure). On the second day the teacher returned and asked whether Valerie fancied helping her organize a reading night for her pupils, a night that the children would spend in the bookshop with the teacher (and the bookseller, of course) and where they'd be allowed to take turns reading. A wonderful idea that was unfortunately quashed by an objection from the school management ('insurance-related reservations').

And yet Valerie summoned up hope, working her way through the area, forging contacts with the other local shops, inviting people to tea, visiting the church, the nearby old-people's home, moving heaven and earth to get her little shop noticed. Meanwhile she kept writing letters. Letters to customers who owed money, to readers who'd ordered or picked up books but hadn't paid. Some, indeed many of these unpaid bills went back years, a number of them even decades. But, undeterred, Valerie typed reminders on Aunt Charlotte's old typewriter. Occasionally she received replies, sometimes even money. A few mortified old customers transferred the money, others included cash with their letters. And after a few weeks the debt level had been reduced from 28,000 euros to just under 27,000.

'Not much,' Valerie mumbled with a frown, examining the address list she'd drawn up. There were only a few of these customers owing money whose addresses she knew or had been able to find out from their correspondence. Taking away all of those with whom she had no idea how to get in contact, and assuming that all those she'd written to and still could write to would duly pay, 'then we're looking at a total of three thousand euros. Just.'

With a sigh she put her head in her hands and her elbows on the typewriter. And while with a 'clack' she kept typing an 'Ä' on the letter she'd just begun, the bell rang and the door opened.

'Hello?'

'I'm here,' Valerie called out, straightening herself, taking a deep breath and practising a professional composure. 'Won't be a sec.'

She ripped out the piece of paper she'd inserted into the typewriter, tossed it into the waste-paper basket (by now she could have joined a district league basketball team at least), stood up and turned to face the visitor.

'You?'

'Have we met?' the visitor asked, letting his gaze roam the shop. 'Where is the owner?'

'I'm . . . Well, erm, I'm standing in for her.' Valerie cleared her throat. 'During her absence.'

'Oh, what a shame. I'd hoped to find her here.' The man scrutinized her inquisitively. A few biscuit crumbs were caught in his beard, his eyebrows arched theatrically above black flashing eyes, with which he virtually skewered Valerie, but not in an unfriendly way. 'So you must be the woman who wrote me this letter?'

It struck Valerie that she ought to take a

deep breath to forestall a medical incident. 'Erm, yes, that was . . . me.'

He nodded and stared at her again. Then his face twisted into an ironic and mischievous smile, and he held out his hand. 'Delighted to meet you. I'm . . . '

'But of course,' Valerie said. 'I know who you are. It's an honour that you've come to pay Ringelnatz & Co. a visit.'

'And you are?'

'Valerie. Call me Valerie.'

'With pleasure.' He took another look around.

'Nothing's changed,' he stated. 'Everything is how I remember. Perhaps even a touch more beautiful. But in those days I didn't have eyes for the shop. Is Charlotte well?'

'Thanks, erm . . . ' Valerie stuttered. 'I hope so. We haven't heard from her in a long time. She's . . . she's been away for quite a while.'

Another smile. 'Yes,' he said, 'that's Charlotte all right. She always had a mind of her own.'

He felt in his pocket and took out a rather tatty envelope. 'First I'm going to give you this to finally settle my debts. I hope it's enough. I'm sure those books you listed weren't all the ones I, well, bought without paying for them. Money is unimportant to me, you know. If one has enough of it, one sometimes forgets just how important it is for other people.'

Valerie took the envelope from his hand. 'I'm sure it's enough,' she said. 'May I offer you a cup of tea?'

'That would be lovely.'

'Perhaps you'd like to take a seat . . . ' She pointed to the comfortable armchair by the window.

'Thanks very much. How marvellous that this old furniture still exists.'

Then the great Noé from Vienna sat down and absentmindedly watched Valerie fill the teapot, looking so unbelievably like her old aunt — a miracle of memory.

★ ★ ★

The famous actor's visit turned out to be the best PR coup imaginable. It was probably pure coincidence that while he was there a middle-aged woman looked in the window and then a bit further into the shop! That she recognized the elderly thespian and her heart missed a beat in sheer ecstasy, before setting into a wild gallop. That she had a mobile on her and phoned her friend without delay, upon which two happy new customers of Ringelnatz & Co. turned up, who surpassed each other in cultural matters (which to

Valerie's delight manifested itself in book purchases). That the friend in question clearly telephoned another friend or several friends and told them. And thus it wasn't long before a group of Viennese female fans had surrounded Noé and were hanging breathlessly on his every word — a mixture of anecdotes from the life of a global star and book recommendations. Not everything was in stock (if we're being honest, Valerie knew neither Thoreau, the author, nor *Walden*, his most important work). But as several copies were urgently needed of almost all the books commended to the gathering of women, the young bookseller started taking orders as if she were offering gold at the price of silver in her shop.

The extraordinary revitalization of the shop did not go unnoticed that afternoon and led to a large number of other visitors, some of whom were unaware that they were breathing the same air as a celebrity as they looked around the shop in amazement and, if only out of embarrassment, bought a couple of cheaper books (although here we should note that it's often the slim and cheaper volumes that harbour the sweetest dreams).

When, as evening approached, the great Noé strained to lift himself from the chair, a collective sigh passed through the group of middle-aged women.

'You know,' he said, 'I could spend hours with you ladies; your company here today has been most enchanting. You are a source of pure joy.' With a consummately gallant bow he kissed the hands of some of his admirers. And if he hadn't given Valerie the odd, barely perceptible wink from time to time she would have regarded the afternoon as a piece of absurd theatre come true. But this made her understand that someone had decided not only to settle an old bill, but to compensate for a longstanding debt.

Never before had Ringelnatz & Co. enjoyed such a rich turnover as in those five hours that the great Noé from Vienna spent in the shop.

14

In the sad month of November, when the days were getting murkier and the wind tore the leaves from the trees, one of the construction workers came over. Valerie had been watching him for a while from her place by the door. She'd wrapped herself in a thick woollen blanket and turned on the samovar, to which she kept returning to fill up her glass (several days earlier she'd gone to the Glestan Market and discovered these gorgeous little tea glasses with a golden rim, out of which the tea, as she soon noticed, tasted quite different, more aromatic, much clearer), opened up a collection of short stories by Anton Chekhov and was spellbound by the story 'Home' — until she noticed that on the scaffolding opposite a middle-aged man, a builder with a sad face, was looking over at her. Was he gazing at her longingly? From this distance she couldn't see properly. Valerie went in to fetch another glass of tea and when she returned to her table, the man turned away and got back down to his work. She sat down, opened the book again and read from the very corner of her eyes, as a friendly autumn sun shone on her forehead.

'Someone came from the Grigoryevs' to fetch a book, but I said you were not at home. The postman brought the newspaper and two letters. By the way, Yevgeny Petrovitch, I should like to ask you to speak to Seryozha. To-day, and the day before yesterday, I have noticed that he is smoking . . .

'Sorry to bother you, Miss . . . '

Valerie got a fright. She'd not heard the man coming. It was the construction worker from over the road. He stood in front of her in his grey clothing, his head slightly bowed and his cap in both hands, like someone out of a Victor Hugo novel.

'No, that's fine.' She put her book down and made to stand up.

'I'm really sorry. I don't want to . . . '

'Honestly, don't worry. How can I help you?'

'It's just . . . ' He was waging an internal battle. Was it excessive politeness, was it timidity? 'I've seen you drinking tea.' He cleared his throat and Valerie noticed his small hands. 'And so I thought maybe I can get a glass from you. Obviously I'll pay.'

'Well, this is actually a bookshop here. Tea . . . ' She threw back the blanket and stood up. It really was cold. An earnest wind gusted down the street. It must be freezing up on the scaffolding. 'Of course,' Valerie said. 'A glass of tea. Very happy to get you one.' She pointed to her chair. 'Take a seat,' she said, before biting her lip because she instantly regretted it — now he'd sit with his filthy work clothes on her favourite blanket and . . .

But he waved his hand dismissively. 'No thanks, that's not necessary. Just a glass of tea. From up there I saw that you have a samovar. It reminds me of my country.'

Valerie nodded, went inside and came out shortly afterwards with a glass of tea and some sugar. 'There you are,' she said, handing him the honey-coloured, steaming drink. The man shoved his cap into his coat pocket and seized the glass. Not greedily, but with a gesture that reminded Valerie of a religious ritual.

'You make such nice tea,' he said with a gentle sigh. 'Dark, strong — how it ought to be. Most people in this country make tea too weak. It has no aroma, it has no taste. In my country we say, 'It's seen a policeman.''

'Seen a policeman?'

'Because it's turned so pale.'

Valerie nodded with a smile. Why on earth was this man working on the construction site? His dark eyes sparkled; in the corners sat mischief as well as a touch of sadness.

'Which is your home country?' Valerie

asked, studying his features.

'Persia,' he said, taking a little sip of tea and another, and listening to his word repeating itself in Valerie's voice:

'Persia. Have you been living here long?'

'Too long. Thank you for the tea! It's delicious.' He finished the glass in small sips, before putting it on the table and reaching inside his pocket.

'No money, please. It's my treat,' Valerie said, holding up her hand.

'I cannot accept that,' the man insisted, shaking his head.

'If it's reminded you of home then for me that's payment enough.' Valerie gave him a friendly smile and he shrugged.

'That is terribly kind of you, thanks.' He nodded at the window. 'You're a bookseller,' he said.

'Yes, I am.'

'A lovely bookshop. My uncle had one in Shiraz.'

'Shiraz? I assume that's a town in Persia.'

'It is. The greatest writers came from there. Hafez. Saadi.'

'I believe we have books by both of them here,' said Valerie, indicating the door. 'Actually the bookshop belongs to my aunt.'

Wistfully, the man gazed at the entrance. 'There is nothing more beautiful than a bookshop. I wish you had Persian books here too.'

'As I said, we've definitely got Hafez. Shall I take a look?' Valerie was making for the door but the man shook his head. 'Do you know what? Hafez isn't easy even in Persian. I would never understand it in German.' He appeared deep in thought for a moment, then continued, 'But maybe you could recommend me a good book in German that's not so difficult.'

'Wait, I'll be right back.' She took the blanket off the chair and, with a swift gesture, invited him finally to sit down, before going into the shop. When she returned soon afterwards she held out a slim volume, bound in black leather and with embossed golden letters that spelled: *Peter Schlemihl*.

The man opened it and read:

After a favourable, but for me most onerous passage, we finally reached the harbour. As soon as the boat and I had landed ashore, I loaded up my few pos-sessions . . .

He looked up. 'How enchanting. You Germans write so beautifully.'

'This book was written by a Frenchman,' Valerie explained. 'But in German. His name was Adelbert von Chamisso. It's called *Peter Schlemihl's Miraculous Story*, a very special book.'

The man nodded, shut it and ran the tips of his slender fingers along the binding. 'If he wrote it in German, I must be able to read it in German. I will try. How much is it?'

Valerie told him the price, he paid, bowed a final time then hurried back to the building site, where he was soon on the scaffolding again, dragging timbers and tightening clamps, a world away from Chamisso or Hafez. But Valerie took her things inside and looked for the great Persian writer in her aunt's card index. *Love Poems*. Only a small book, similar to the one she had given the builder, but richly decorated. She opened it at random, as she liked to do with poetry books, because sometimes — although only if she liked the result — she read them like an oracle:

I received the happy news
That these days of sorrow will not
last,
That it will not remain as it was
And not remain as it is now.

She paused. Is that what she wanted?

★　★　★

One Saturday — at this point we should note that Valerie was not especially disciplined about keeping to opening hours, but on that day she happened to be there — the Persian was standing at the door, knocking with a politeness that bordered on timidity.

'I don't wish to disturb you,' he hurried to assure Valerie, when he saw her standing with a list at the non-fiction shelf.

'You're not disturbing me at all, please come in!'

'It's just that I discovered a book you might like.' With a bow typical of him he handed her a parcel wrapped in simple packing paper. 'It's by a Persian. It appeared first in English, but this here is a German translation.'

'Well now,' Valerie said, offering him her warmest smile, 'you've pricked my curiosity. Many thanks! I'll give you it back when I've finished.'

'No, no, no!' he said, holding up his hands. 'You don't have to do that. It's a present. I'm very happy when I can explain to other people how hard life is in my country.'

Valerie nodded. 'I understand. Now then . . . ' She'd already started to turn around when the Persian thought of something else. 'If you like, rather than pay for the book, come to the

141

theatre. There is a group of students who are putting on a play. This evening. It is the story of this book. And I think they've done it very well. You would be doing a good thing if you bought a ticket. For these young people are very courageous. I'll leave you a flyer.'

As if attempting to forestall her rejection he hurriedly pulled a red flyer from his pocket and placed it on top of the package in Valerie's hands. Then he bowed again and disappeared so quickly that any response would have been pointless.

A touch disconcerted, but mainly curious, the young woman went into the office, put the parcel on the desk, grabbed the letter opener and carefully cut through the sticky tape. The name of the author stood there like an exotic promise: Shahriar Mandanipour. When she took the book out of its package the title sounded so confusing she had to read it twice: *Censoring an Iranian Love Story*. Her gaze wandered to the red theatre flyer peeking out from beneath the wrapping paper. The production it advertised had a different title: *Teheran, Mon Amour*.

The novel was the story of a Persian writer who — as became clear to Valerie after a few pages — was prevented by circumstances from publishing a love story in his own language, because love and passion were considered the

142

devil's work in his country, and everything that corresponds to the beautiful, good and true is turned on its head.

In the air of Tehran, the scent of spring blossoms, carbon monoxide, and the perfumes and poisons of the tales of One Thousand and One Nights sway on top of each other, they whisper together. The city drifts in time . . .

Valerie learned that publishing love stories in Iran is no simple endeavour. 'Endeavour,' Valerie thought — a beautiful word that might appeal to the Persian construction worker. In Iran you are allowed to publish and print these sorts of stories. But to sell them you need the approval of the Ministry of Culture and Islamic Guidance. In this government department, however, sits a gentleman with the nickname Petrovich (that's right, Detective Porfiry Petrovich, who has to investigate Raskolnikov's murder in Dostoevsky's *Crime and Punishment*). His job is to read books assiduously, novels and stories, love stories in particular . . . He crosses out every word, every sentence, every paragraph and even whole pages if they are indecent and consequently represent a danger to public morals and time-honoured social values.

143

The play was performed in the basement of an old house in the city centre, instead of in a conventional theatre. Perhaps there was no stage for this sort of thing over there. The entire company consisted of only four students, all of whom acted with such virtuosity and ease that Valerie was enthralled by the performance, in which the oppression of a great and ancient people was dramatized with colourful ideas and delightful entanglements until it became a comedy as bittersweet as oriental tea.

She saw the Persian construction worker too. He was sitting in a corner at the very back, where he didn't stand out. Dressed in a smart suit and freshly shaven, he could have been taken for a doctor or a lawyer, one of the old-fashioned types. Perhaps he was a doctor, Valerie pondered as she looked at him covertly. Who could say what reasons had caused him to leave his country and what unfortunate chain of events had driven him to scaffolding and cement mixers? Valerie thought about the character of Sara in *Censoring An Iranian Love Story*. Like Valerie, Sara was a student, but her studies had been so different. There had been a passage in which Sara tried to borrow a book called *The Blind Owl* from the university library and was told the book was banned. Valerie couldn't imagine living in a place where certain books were forbidden.

But a young man has been watching her in the library and he will find ways and means of getting her that book. And with the book a message that he'll pass on to her in a secret code. This develops into a forbidden love story — above all, the telling of the story is forbidden. For books, as Valerie learned, are dangerous in a country where freedom doesn't exist.

And so that evening Valerie went back to her bookshop deep in thought (she'd intended to go home, but then decided to check whether *The Blind Owl* actually existed: it did). The book the Persian construction worker had given her was still on the little table beside the armchair. Valerie stroked the cover, picked it up and read some passages of the text she'd just heard in the basement as part of a tightly packed audience. How animated such a text is, how directly it can be translated into action.

★　★　★

The worker from Persia, whose name was Aghaye Massoud, visited on a few other

145

occasions, until one day his team had finished the tasks assigned to them there and they were sent on to their next job, or the weather made it impossible to continue working. For at some point, of course, it had become wintry. An unpleasant wind howled down the street, darkness alternated with the murk of late-autumn and early-winter days, snow with rain. On one of the last sunny days, close to the start of Advent, Valerie again dared to put her table outside and present herself to the dazzling, oblique sun. She was going to miss this ritual she'd been performing since late summer and thanks to which she'd enjoyed so many journeys around the world. With Highgrown Kenya tea she'd followed Piscine Molitor Patel's experiences with the intuitive Bengal tiger Richard Parker in the expanses of the Pacific Ocean; with English Breakfast she'd studied *Jin Ping Mei*'s China; with Gunpowder she'd giggled at *The Innocents Abroad*. With Tippy Golden Flowery Orange Pekoe she'd traced the fate of *The Beautiful Mrs Seidenmann* through the streets of Warsaw; Sencha had accompanied her to the Swiss Alps and *The Magic Mountain*; Lapsang Souchong on *A Passage to India*; Darjeeling from the highest plantations of the Himalayas on John Franklin's search for the Northwest Passage; an East Frisian blend

146

through the backwater of Macondo in the Columbian Jungle; and Peruvian Mate with *The Aspern Papers* through the melancholy alleys of Venice.

A number of discoveries were thanks to Aghaye, who turned out to be a very well-read and sophisticated man. Valerie missed him as she had missed Timmi (although not as much, because, although the boy had been a touch mysterious, he was nowhere near as polite and reserved). And so the gloomy, rainy autumn days departed and winter set in. One day a letter arrived — from Timmi. In tidy, error-free handwriting and in light-blue ink he wrote:

Dear bookseller,
We moved, unfortunately. That's why I can't come by any more. But I still owe you money. So I've put four euros in this envelope. I hope this letter gets to you. And I hope you're well. Sadly, there's no bookshop on the way to my new school. But if I'm in the area again I'll pop by. All the best!
Regards,

Timmi

Valerie was touched. There were four euros in the envelope. The boy had paid off his debt. The accounts tallied. His letter pulled at her heartstrings — how could it not? Valerie didn't need to mull it over for long. She'd given the construction worker over the road a special book as a goodbye present. Now she wrapped the same book in tissue paper — Timmi would be highly appreciative of this — and wrote him a card:

Dear Timmi,
Coincidentally this book costs exactly
four euros in my shop. Perhaps you'll
like it. It's not especially beautiful —
from the outside. But inside it's a trea-
sure chest! Visit me if you're ever in the
area. I'll always have a cup of tea for
you.
All the best,

Valerie

She placed the card in an envelope, wrote down the return address that Timmi had put on the back of his envelope and carefully inserted the book. She could see him virtually sinking into the text, this sensitive, precocious boy; she could see him with his nose over the book, listening carefully to the echo of the early morning in the luxuriant growth of the woodland solitude and feeling the travel bug in the swarm of words in this foliage: *The Unfolding of Language*. A book, not especially beautiful to look at, but a treasure trove of linguistic delicacies, the like of which you might not find anywhere else.

★   ★   ★

As Christmas approached business picked up again a little, but towards the end of the year it practically came to a halt. Occasionally one or other of the middle-aged women would come in, presumably in the hope that the famous actor might be there. But in the icily cold days leading up to New Year very few customers graced the small bookshop. And at the start of the following year the financial situation was scarcely better than when Valerie had taken on the business. When she opened up in the morning she was greeted by worry and when she locked up in the evening despair waved goodbye to her. Without her small flights of literature, she might have given up. But if you know you're doing the right thing and you really love it, you'll accept many a hardship and many a disappointment. And then there was that letter from Italy.

15

On the very anniversary of the elderly bookseller's disappearance a letter came in the post, written on paper from the Albergo d'Angelini in Florence and sealed in one of the hotel's envelopes. In the shaky hand of an old lady, but penned with great care to produce a charming script, the following words had been written:

Dear Valerie,
I hope my letter arrives punctually and that you're well. It's now time for me finally to take back the burden I placed on you. I wonder whether much has changed. I'm looking forward to seeing you. Perhaps you'd be so kind as to meet me at the station. I'm arriving on Tuesday at 11.50 on platform 7.
Love,

Charlotte

That was it. Nothing else. Confused, Valerie looked at the calendar: Tuesday. And the time: just after eleven. Did Aunt

Charlotte mean this Tuesday: today?

If the old lady had possessed a mobile it would have been simple to clear up the matter. But even if she did have one (which Valerie doubted) Valerie didn't have the number. And actually, she could have telephoned Valerie herself at some point, just as she could have let her family know for certain that nothing bad had happened to her when she vanished into thin air, that she was keeping well and ultimately had just been following a crazy whim, or at least fulfilling an obligation that Valerie might have understood had she explained. But nothing of the sort had happened. She had simply absconded in the dead of night, leaving behind no more than a few dry words which were all that suggested her disappearance might at least have been intentional. And now she was announcing her return with a few similarly dry words — and it was imminent.

Valerie scrunched up both letter and envelope, and tossed them in the direction of the waste-paper basket. She was disappointed. She was resentful. And no, she wasn't going to pick up the old lady from the station. Anyway, even if she'd wanted to, she'd barely have made it. She'd have had to leave straightaway. She'd have needed a taxi. She'd barely have had time to put on her coat, throw money, mobile, keys into her bag and lock the door behind her. She'd barely have been able to glance at Grisaille, who gave her a look of astonishment, and whose whiskers seemed to be swirling around a smile.

It was pure coincidence that a taxi stopped on the other side of the road at that very moment. Or a sign. More automatically than intentionally, Valerie waved from the door. The driver had a trained eye. He flashed his lights and turned round. Valerie grabbed her things, locked up behind her and got in. She was no longer surprised to find that the taxi was quicker than she'd expected (and more expensive). But perhaps it only seemed like that because on the way she absolutely had to finish reading Balzac's *The Wild Ass's Skin*. At any rate she found herself so suddenly at the main entrance to the station that she first had to get her bearings.

Platform 7. To her surprise the train was already there. A glance at her watch told her that it was only a quarter to twelve. The first passengers were alighting. Trolleys were pushed past, couples embraced, a stubborn child howled while its mother grumbled as she looked around. A line of chained-up baggage trolleys stood in the way, a man walked past Valerie and offered her a James

Bond smile. An elderly lady stood slightly to one side. Valerie trotted a few paces up to her, but then realized that it wasn't Aunt Charlotte. She moved slowly forwards so as not to miss her. She noticed as she walked past it that the first carriage was already empty. Soon afterwards, the entire train appeared to have been vacated; no one else was coming out. Valerie stopped and looked at the huge vehicle. All the passengers had been disgorged. All of them? Valerie got on and walked along the empty rows of a carriage, then the next one and the one after that, all the while keeping an eye on the windows facing the platform, so that the old lady didn't slip past her outside in the opposite direction. But that didn't happen.

Valerie had reached the first-class compartments that made up the end of the train. Nothing. This carriage was abandoned too. She was about to turn around and get off when she caught sight of a small book that had been left on one of the tables. It looked familiar so she stepped closer. A hunch crept over her. She picked the book up and stroked the front cover. It was beautifully bound in half linen, with an embossed title and even a ribbon marker in hopeful green.

She instinctively looked up at the seat numbers: 13. A glance at the end of the carriage confirmed it was number 12. Baffled, Valerie sank into the seat and opened the book with her trembling fingers. It came as no surprise to be greeted by the words:

There had been no forewarning of the sudden change in weather

Nor did it come as a surprise to find an envelope in the book. No address, no writing at all on it. The envelope was unsealed. Lifting the flap, Valerie took out the contents: two train tickets that had remained passably dry. First class, Valerie noted. They were for today. Two tickets to Paris. Seat 13 and — seat 13. Puzzled, she looked at the numbers above the seats. Two tickets for seat 13? Impossible. And yet there it was on the ticket in black and white: Carriage 12, Seat 13, both times. Until she realized what she'd realized when reading that same book before tossing it into the recycling: only the first ticket was for Paris. The second was from Paris to . . .

★   ★   ★

Maybe everything would have turned out differently if at that moment Valerie hadn't looked out and spied Aunt Charlotte, sitting on a bench with her hands on an umbrella, smiling at her. The old woman nodded and

154

with her head indicated the display above the platform, which now, enticingly, bore the destination Paris-Est. Maybe everything really would have turned out differently had not a young man appeared next to her — as if from nowhere — wearing an elegant, if somewhat old-fashioned between-seasons coat, from the pocket of which the headlines of the *Frankfurter Allgemeine Zeitung* poked out nosily; a rather creased shirt, with spectacles in the breast pocket; and Italian shoes, which may no longer have been brand new, but were well looked after.

'You have your own copy,' he said, gesturing to the book in Valerie's hands. '*A Very Special Year.*'

Valerie nodded. 'The book you spent so long hunting for in vain because only a few copies of it exist,' she said, opening it and turning two, three pages. All of a sudden she knew what would happen if she turned the page again. She glanced at the two tickets in her hand. Paris. And . . .

'Stockholm?' the young man asked.

Valerie looked outside, where the bench stood empty.

'Wherever!' the young man exclaimed. 'Do you mind if I sit down?' He didn't wait for her answer. 'A magic book in the truest sense of the word. I remember you thought it was a defective copy. Didn't you know it was your own book?'

'And yet you took it with you.'

'The fact that I found it at your shop meant above all that it found me there,' he said softly. 'And you hadn't even discovered the tickets.'

Valerie nodded. 'Yes, I really did think the whole thing had been misprinted. I mean only a few pages had text on them.' Of course she had realized some time ago what the book signified.

The young man shrugged his shoulders. 'It simply wasn't the right time for you to continue reading. But now things seem to be different, otherwise you wouldn't be on this train. Otherwise Destiny would not have gifted you another copy.'

'Quite clearly so. Do you think the book's magic will reveal itself to me?'

'I'm sure it will.'

At that moment she heard the guard's whistle. She looked up. The young man's dark eyes were staring mysteriously at her.

'Don't you have to get out?' she asked.

'What, now that our stories have brought us together? *Send me word that you permit me to come and offer to you my servitude: for if you do not, and that quickly, you'll be accused of having inhumanely killed without* a cause of all your servants the most passionate, the most humble, and the most obedient servant.'

Valerie gave him a smile. 'Cyrano?'

The young man nodded. And in a flash she made a decision: she would go. To Paris and thence to . . . She turned the page and . . . yes, it was no longer blank — the book told a story. The story of a very special year. A year such as the old woman had lived and as the young man had lived, albeit in a very different way. She would likewise experience her very own story.

'London,' she read and nodded dreamily. 'A book that tells each person their own story?'

'At any rate a book that each person reads and understands differently,' the young man replied. 'It really is a magical book.'

Looking up at him she saw that he was gazing at her with curiosity in his eyes. Of course he couldn't know this, but *she* did: she'd already lived through her very special year. In that tiny bookshop, but especially in the numerous books and stories that she'd read since taking over her unexpected duty. There was *one* book she hadn't read. The most mysterious of all. Well, now it lay before her. And as the train rolled slowly out of the station, she placed her hand on that of the young man and finally started to read her story. At the end of the year would she, like Aunt Charlotte, return to this same place? She didn't know. But she did know for whom she'd put two tickets into the book, one to Prague, perhaps, and one to Tehran.

Yes, maybe everything would have turned out differently on that winter's day if literature hadn't given a young lady wings. But in this way Valerie made a decision that would change everything, not least — in fact this most of all — her whole life.

Epilogue

I'm sure you'd like to know how the story ends. Well, the elderly lady who once upon a time founded a business with her budding dreams, only to lead it into ruin, lovingly and with unswerving effort, is back. Meanwhile, the young, hopeful, business economist, who has discovered her love for literature over the year, ditched a useless boyfriend and sparked a passion in a number of new readers, has departed the stage and — who knows? — maybe will never return . . . But we need not worry about Valerie; quite clearly she hasn't found love in only the world of books. Of course, the old bookshop might up sticks to a new location where people have a greater appreciation of culture and are also prepared to spend a bit of money on it from time to time. It is also highly possible that one of the large chains of bookshops will take the little business under its wing and under the group's name lead it to new revenue. Another possibility, however, is that in the not-too-distant future the last of the money will run out and thus what was looming at the beginning of our short story, the liquidation of Ringelnatz & Co., will finally occur after all. There aren't many other options, although there's definitely one. But ultimately it depends on you. Because, of course, there is such a nursery for budding dreams near you too. Or, to finish on a truism: Ringelnatz & Co. is everywhere.

We do hope that you have enjoyed reading this large print book.

Did you know that all of our titles are available for purchase?

We publish a wide range of high quality large print books including:
Romances, Mysteries, Classics
General Fiction
Non Fiction and Westerns

Special interest titles available in large print are:
The Little Oxford Dictionary
Music Book
Song Book
Hymn Book
Service Book

Also available from us courtesy of Oxford University Press:
Young Readers' Dictionary
(large print edition)
Young Readers' Thesaurus
(large print edition)

For further information or a free brochure, please contact us at:
Ulverscroft Large Print Books Ltd.,
The Green, Bradgate Road, Anstey,
Leicester, LE7 7FU, England.
Tel: (00 44) 0116 236 4325
Fax: (00 44) 0116 234 0205

Other titles published by Ulverscroft:

LOOK AT ME

Sarah Duguid

Lizzy lives with her father Julian and her brother Ig in North London. Two years ago her mother died, leaving a family bereft by her absence and a house still filled with her things. Margaret was lively, beautiful, fun, loving — as far as Lizzy is concerned, she kept the family together. Then, one day, Lizzy finds a letter from a stranger to her father, and discovers he has another child. In an act of outraged defiance, Lizzy invites this new half-sister into her family's world — and, almost immediately, realises her mistake . . .